Pistols at Red River
Andrew Jackson v. Charles Dickinson

Allen Sircy

Copyright © 2026 Allen Sircy
All rights reserved. No part of this publication may be reproduced, distributed, or transmitted in any form or by any means, including photocopying, recording, or other electronic or mechanical methods, without the prior written permission of the publisher, except in the case of brief quotations embodied in critical reviews and certain other noncommercial uses permitted by copyright law.

Published by Southern Ghost Stories, Gallatin, Tennessee

ISBN: 979-8-9988146-6-2

Table of Contents

Prologue 5

The Ball 8

The Wager 10

"A Damn Equivocator" 24

Satisfaction 40

Unobstructed 50

"A Lady in Every Respect" 57

"I Shall Have His Life" 70

The Bar of Honor 83

Goodbye 97

Buzzards 104

"Fire!" 111

"From Dust We Came" 128

"Some Wounds" 141

Author's Note 145

Prologue

July 24, 1788, Harrodsburg, Kentucky

The wagon creaked to a stop in front of the boarding house. Samuel Donelson climbed down and stood for a moment, taking in the modest place. *Temporary*, he thought. It was the kind of place you stayed when there was nowhere else to go. He straightened his coat and stepped inside.

The smell hit him first—whiskey and sweat, mixed with stale air. Lewis Robards stood near the table, broad-shouldered and red-faced with a glass in his hand. His eyes flicked to Samuel and stayed there. Samuel forced a smile. "Lewis."

Lewis didn't return it.

"I've come to collect Rachel's belongings," Samuel said, his voice calm and measured. "I don't wish to quarrel." Lewis merely snorted and took a drink.

A chair scraped softly in the corner as John Overton closed his book and rose. He was gentle-faced and neatly dressed, the sort of man who could calm the tempers in a room just by standing in it. "Samuel," Overton said. "My friend, it is good to see you."

Samuel managed a warmer smile. "John."

"I'll help you," Overton said, already moving down the hall. Lewis watched them go, saying nothing. Overton stopped at the last door and knocked. Rachel opened it, her shoulders tight and her eyes cautious.

"Your brother is here," Overton said kindly.

Rachel didn't look surprised; she had been waiting. When Overton asked if he could help with anything, she simply pointed to a scuffed, heavy trunk in the corner. He nodded. "Of course."

As Rachel stepped into the main room, the boarding house went quiet. Doors opened and faces appeared; women lingered in doorways and a man leaned against the banister, but no one spoke. Lewis sat down hard in a chair, his glass waiting for him on the table. He picked it up and drank as Samuel crossed the room to wrap his arms around his sister. She held him tightly, just for a second, then let go.

Overton gestured toward the hallway. "Lewis, would you help us with the trunk?"

Lewis stared at him, long and hostile, then turned away. He sank deeper into his chair and lifted the glass again. Samuel exhaled. "I'll help."

Together, Overton and Samuel carried the trunk out. It strained them both; they bumped the frame and cursed under their breath before finally wrestling it onto the wagon. Rachel stood outside, hands clasped, eyes fixed on the trunk as if it might be taken back at the last moment.

"Ready to go home?" Samuel asked, wiping his palms on his trousers. She nodded just once, then turned and hugged Overton.

At the door, Rachel stopped. Lewis hadn't moved. She wiped at her face, her voice trembling slightly. "Is this truly what you want?" He said nothing. She swallowed hard. "Goodbye, Lewis."

Still nothing. She stepped forward anyway. "I wish you well."

Lewis finally looked at her, his voice flat. "Go on. Get out of here."

The tears came then, silent. Samuel and Overton

appeared at her side without a word, guiding her to the wagon. Overton helped her climb up. "I'll see that the divorce papers are filed with the court," he promised. "Properly."

"Thank you," Rachel replied.

"I wish you safe travels. I'll see you soon."

Samuel shook his hand, and Overton watched as the wagon pulled away. The road stretched ahead, trees blurring past as they left the boarding house behind. Samuel glanced at his sister. "Don't fret over him. We'll get you home." She looked out toward the road, let out a slow breath, and wiped at her cheek.

After a beat, Samuel added casually, as if mentioning the weather, "Mother knows a young attorney she wants you to meet." Rachel didn't turn. "His name's Andrew Jackson."

The wagon rolled on.

The Ball

January 29, 1835, Washington D.C.

The night air was thick and damp as Wilson Sneed hurried up the path of the Executive Mansion, his breath ragged and his coat flapping behind him. The lights inside burned late, too late. He reached the front door and barely had time to straighten his clothes before it swung open.

Sarah Jackson stood there, worry written plainly across her face. "Please, come in," she said at once. "President Jackson is in a great deal of pain. He is upstairs."

"I came as quickly as I could, ma'am," Sneed replied, already stepping into the hall.

She led him through the mansion and up the stairs. Sneed tried not to stare, but the place carried a gravity all its own. Sarah stopped at a bedroom door and pushed it open. Andrew Jackson lay propped against the pillows, seventy years carved deep into his face. Even at rest, he looked unyielding. He shifted, clearly uncomfortable.

"The doctor is here," Sarah said.

"I told you I'd be fine, dear," Jackson replied, forcing himself up onto an elbow. "My daughter-in-law worries too much." Sarah rolled her eyes but said nothing.

Sneed stepped forward. "President Jackson, I'm Dr. Wilson Sneed. I am here to help. Tell me, sir, are you in pain?"

"Please," Jackson said with a faint, stubborn smile, "call me Andrew." He grimaced slightly and tapped a finger against his chest.

"Can you please lift your shirt for me?" Sneed asked.

Jackson sat up and pulled the fabric aside. Sneed caught his breath. An old scar, pale and puckered, sat low on the left side of Jackson's chest, angry even after decades. "Oh my, what happened here?" Sneed asked quietly.

Jackson chuckled. "A young man shot me nearly thirty years ago."

Sneed stared. "Was the ball removed?"

"No." The word landed heavy in the room.

"And you're not in constant pain?"

"Only now and then," Jackson said. "At times when the weather is cold."

Sneed reached into his bag and produced a small vial. "This is laudanum. It should help."

Jackson waved it away and glanced at Sarah in the doorway. "Sarah, would you go fetch me that whiskey from downstairs?"

She hesitated. "I don't think…"

"My dear," Jackson cut in, "I am the President of the United States."

Sarah sighed and left the room, her footsteps echoing down the stairs. Sneed cleared his throat, waiting for the door to click shut before asking, "May I ask why the man shot you?"

Jackson smiled, his eyes growing distant. "I believe it was in 1805. October, if I recall correctly," he said. "I was at Clover Bottom, it was a horse track in Nashville…" His voice trailed off, already drifting backward through time.

The Wager

November 18, 1805, Nashville, Tennessee

The late autumn sun hung higher than it ought to have over Clover Bottom. It was warm for the season, turning the race track into a bright ribbon of dust and trampled grass. Two stallions thundered down the straightaway, neck and neck, their hooves striking in a hard, rhythmic drumming that carried all the way to the rail where Andrew Jackson stood watching.

At thirty-nine, Jackson was tall, spare, and rigid with the authority of a man long accustomed to being obeyed. A former senator and judge, he now commanded as Major General of the Tennessee militia; even at leisure, he looked as though he were waiting for a challenge. Beside him stood John Overton, steady and composed. He was a man whose calm demeanor mirrored his seat on the Tennessee Supreme Court.

Behind them, the sound of wagon wheels crunched over stone and dirt. A carriage pulled up and stopped, and Joseph Erwin climbed down first. Fifty-something and prosperous, Erwin carried himself like the world had been specially built to make room for him. He was followed by Thomas Swann, a man younger by decades, wiry and eager. Swann carried Erwin's gloves and hat like a servant dressed in a lawyer's coat, hovering a few steps behind, hungry to be noticed.

Erwin approached Overton with easy confidence. "Judge Overton," he said, offering a hand. "It is always a pleasure, sir. How are things on the bench?"

Overton returned the handshake with practiced

warmth. Erwin's eyes then slid to Jackson, his smile sharpening as he extended his hand again. "General Jackson. It is nice to see you."

Jackson took the hand. The exchange was polite, but it wasn't soft.

Out on the track, a jockey led a beautiful black stallion toward the starting area. The horse tossed its head, glossy and proud. Swann watched the two older men like a scavenger waiting for an opening in a conversation he didn't deserve to be in. Erwin tilted his chin toward the black horse. "What do you think about Ploughboy out there?"

A moment of silence followed. It was just long enough to feel intentional. Overton glanced at Jackson, who held the beat, weighing exactly how much honesty Erwin could tolerate.

"Ploughboy is one of the most handsome stallions I've ever seen," Jackson said at last.

Swann nodded hard, too fast, as if trying to borrow Jackson's authority by agreeing with him. But Erwin had already shifted his attention back to the dirt, watching Ploughboy break into motion with a smooth, controlled power.

"That horse never loses," Erwin said, the boast disguised as a casual observation. "Do you know how much money I've won with him?"

Swann couldn't help himself. "An impressive amount, no doubt, Mr. Erwin."

Erwin didn't even turn his head. He kept his focus on Jackson. He was the only audience that mattered. Overton watched the horse; Jackson watched Erwin. Jackson, who had no use for flattery, let the silence sit for one more beat before choosing his words with surgical care.

"Joe," Jackson began, "I don't mean to offend…" He looked out at the stallion, then back, his eyes narrowing. "It seems to me ol' Ploughboy has lost his pace."

Swann's eager grin died as if someone had slapped it off his face. Erwin's expression hardened instantly. "That's nonsense. Have you ever seen him lose a race?"

Jackson tapped his chin thoughtfully. "I can't say that I have."

Erwin seized the opening like it proved his entire existence. "Your friend Mr. Cannon told me Tin Soldier was going to run Ploughboy off the track in Gallatin." He reached into his pocket and pulled out a thick wad of bank notes, fanning them just enough to make the point. "You see this? Ploughboy beat him in two straight heats." He slid the money back into his pocket with a smirk of satisfaction. "I'd go back and race him again this weekend, but Jane and her new husband are coming in from Maryland."

Jackson didn't react to the money or the mention of his friend. He simply kept pushing, the way he always did when he smelled a weakness. "Now Joe, please… Ploughboy is a fine horse." He paused, then let the real line land. "I just don't think he could beat Truxton."

At the mention of Truxton, Swann gave a small, involuntary chuckle, more reflex than judgment. He caught himself and went still. He could read a room; he just couldn't resist testing it.

Erwin gave a short, unfriendly laugh. "Truxton?"

Jackson didn't flinch. Erwin's eyes searched for a crack he could pry open. "Didn't he lose to Greyhound last summer?"

"It's true," Jackson said, not dodging the fact. "But after I took over his training and hired a new jockey, he has yet to be defeated. When we raced against Greyhound again, it was not close."

Overton nodded, backing Jackson without speaking. Jackson let himself smirk, just briefly, before leaning in. He hadn't come to Clover Bottom to admire horses. "What do you say, Joe… Truxton and Ploughboy next Saturday? We can do it here at Clover Bottom."

Erwin studied him, weighing whether this was bravado or certainty. "What are we racing for?"

Jackson's voice didn't rise. "I have six hundred and forty acres along the Cumberland, just north of here. Truxton and I won it from Mr. Cotton a few months ago."

Erwin laughed outright. Overton, sensing the danger, nudged Jackson with the smallest movement of warning. "Do you think Rachel will protest?" Overton asked lightly. "I thought you were going to build her niece a house on the site."

Jackson didn't look away from Erwin. "She'll never know it was even a consideration. Truxton has won seven straight contests." He pointed toward Erwin's pocket. "How much do you have there? I'll put up the property if you'll wager those notes you got from Mr. Cannon."

Erwin dug out the wad again, counting it with his thumb. "It's three hundred dollars."

Jackson didn't blink. "How about that plus three hundred more? Next Saturday at noon. Is that satisfactory?" He extended his hand, decisive, as if the deal were already done and Erwin were simply catching up.

Erwin took the hand, sealing it, and started to turn

away, already tasting the victory.

"Oh... one further matter," Jackson added. Erwin stopped and looked back. "If you or Ploughboy are not here on Saturday, I will demand eight hundred dollars for the forfeit."

Swann's eyebrows lifted, impressed despite himself. Jackson wasn't just wagering; he was tightening a noose. Erwin's surprise smoothed into a smirk. "Agreed. However, when I arrive and do not find *you* here, I trust you will do the same."

"Of course. Eight hundred dollars. You have my word."

Erwin slipped an arm around Overton with mock camaraderie, treating the Supreme Court judge like a prop. "Will you please help the General get those deeds in perfect order for me? See to it my name is spelled correctly. It's E-R-W-I-N."

Overton smiled politely, giving him nothing. Swann leaned toward Erwin and whispered, "Ploughboy will win it, easy enough," before hurrying after him, still clutching the gloves and hat. As they walked away, Swann glanced back over his shoulder, still looking for a shred of approval from the men at the rail.

Jackson watched them go with a grin that didn't reach his eyes. Overton exhaled slowly. "Andrew, that's quite the wager..."

"Truxton will be ready," Jackson said, unsoftened.

"Ploughboy has never lost at this track, Andrew," Overton pressed.

Jackson scoffed, a short, humorless sound. "There's a beginning to all things."

They moved back to the rail. Out on the course, the horses thundered past again, hooves drumming against the packed earth. Jackson watched them closely now — not as a spectator, but as a man already measuring the distance between a win and a catastrophe.

♦ ♦ ♦ ♦ ♦ ♦

A few mornings later, the air in West Nashville was cool and damp. Joseph Erwin descended the back steps of his mansion, pausing to watch several of his horses run the adjacent field. Their breath hung in faint, ghostly plumes as they stretched their legs below the rise of his opulent home.

At the foot of the stairs stood Uncle Bob. The middle-aged servant held a bucket of water in one hand and clutched his hat nervously in the other, wearing a forced brightness that didn't quite reach his eyes.

"Uncle Bob," Erwin said, adjusting his coat against the morning chill, "how's Ploughboy looking? Big race tomorrow."

Uncle Bob hesitated, just a fraction of a second too long. It was enough to betray him. "Well, sir… he wasn't running like he normally does. I had the farrier reshoe him."

Erwin stopped walking. His eyes narrowed, sensing the shape of a problem he hadn't invited. "And he's taking to the new shoes," Erwin said, the words weighted more like a command than a question. "Is he not?"

Uncle Bob shifted his weight, his gaze dropping to the dirt.

"Is he not?" Erwin's voice sharpened.

Silence stretched between them.

"Bob?"

Uncle Bob swallowed hard. "Sir... Ploughboy's got thrush in his back hooves."

The words landed like a lead ball. Erwin straightened, his face flushing a deep, sudden crimson as anger surged up unchecked. Uncle Bob fidgeted with his hat, bracing himself for the storm.

"We cleaned the infection out!" Bob rushed to add, his voice rising in a desperate bid for calm. "But he needs rest, sir. A few weeks, at least. Maybe a month."

Erwin stared at him as though sheer force of will might undo the biological reality of the infection.

"I... I can get Jolly Jim ready," Bob offered quickly, his eyes searching Erwin's face. "Or Leviathan. Both fine thoroughbreds, sir."

"No!" Erwin's shout echoed off the stone walls of the mansion. He moved closer, invading the man's space until they were inches apart. "No! No!" His voice cracked with a jagged fury. "No!"

For a brief, dangerous moment, it looked as though he might strike Bob. Instead, Erwin yanked his own hat from his head, hurled it to the ground, and stormed back toward the house without another word. Bob watched him go, finally letting out the breath he'd been holding since dawn.

Inside, the mansion was a sanctuary of polished wood and fine fabrics, but none of the quiet wealth was enough to absorb the violence of Erwin's temper. He snatched a brass candlestick from a side table and flung it across the parlor. It struck the wall with a sharp crack before clattering onto the floorboards.

Jane Dickinson rushed in first, her skirts gathered

in her hands and alarm written on her face. Her husband, Charles, followed close behind. Though handsome and usually self-assured, Charles looked visibly startled by the wreckage.

"Father!" Jane cried. "What is the matter?"

"Is something wrong?" Charles asked.

"Wrong?" Erwin barked, pacing the rug like a caged animal. "I'm in a fix. I entered Ploughboy in a race—and now that damn horse can't run."

Charles winced, trying to inject logic into the room. "You have others just as fast. Could you run Jolly Jim?"

Erwin collapsed onto the couch, the fight draining out of him as quickly as it had arrived. Charles sat beside him, leaning in. "No, Charles," Erwin said bitterly. "I made a wager with General Jackson. I bet three hundred dollars on Ploughboy."

Charles paused, measuring the gravity of the name.

"And if there's a forfeiture," Erwin went on, his voice hollow, "I agreed to pay him eight hundred."

"Perhaps you can postpone the contest," Charles suggested.

Erwin shook his head sharply. "You don't know Andrew Jackson. That bastard will demand payment the moment he sees Ploughboy isn't there. And I don't have the notes to pay him."

Jane tried to soothe him with a hand on his shoulder. "I'm sure it can be settled."

Erwin scoffed, the sound full of contempt.

"I've heard he's a scoundrel," Charles noted. "Didn't he challenge the governor to a duel?"

"Yes," Erwin snapped. "Governor Sevier would've been justified putting a ball straight through his black heart. Jackson has no sense of decency. His mother worked in a house of ill fame, and he married another man's wife."

Jane's mouth fell open. Charles stared, stunned by the vitriol. "What?" Jane whispered. "I thought bigamy was against the law."

"She had a husband in Kentucky," Erwin said, waving a hand as if dismissing a fly, "but Jackson dragged her into the Mississippi Territory where laws don't apply. He's uncouth, but clever."

"And they put that man in charge of the state militia?" Charles asked, incredulous.

Erwin gave a short, humorless laugh. "He curries favor at the racetrack with judges and lawyers, and somehow people think him to be honorable. It's balderdash."

The anger finally vanished, leaving only a cold, lingering dread. Erwin leaned forward and buried his face in his hands. "I'll have to go to the track," he muttered into his palms. "I'll have to speak to him."

Defeated, he stayed there, shoulders slumped, knowing the conversation would not go the way he hoped.

◆◆◆◆◆◆

The next morning, Clover Bottom buzzed with the frantic movement of race day. Horses circled the course in a blur of muscle and sweat while men gathered along the rail, their voices rising over the thundering of hooves. Andrew Jackson stood apart from the crowd, watching Truxton gallop down the track. The horse moved cleanly, every stride a confident strike against the packed earth.

At Jackson's side stood the Overton brothers. John was his usual steady self, while Thomas, short, husky, and slightly aloof, maintained a good-natured but watchful silence.

"Truxton looks unstoppable today," Jackson remarked, his eyes never leaving the horse. "Poor Ploughboy hasn't a chance."

The Overtons nodded in unison. Jackson scanned the grounds, his gaze sharpening as it cut through the crowd. "Has anyone seen Joe? I didn't see Ploughboy in the stable."

John Overton spotted them first. He gave a small, meaningful nod toward Joseph Erwin, who was approaching with Charles Dickinson. Trailing just behind them was Nathaniel McNairy. Only in his early twenties, McNairy was sharp-eyed and carried the effortless self-assurance of a young man who knew his family name held weight in Tennessee. He walked beside Thomas Swann, close enough to look like a confidant, though he kept a calculated distance—observing rather than engaging.

Jackson noticed the shift in the air immediately. Erwin had his hat in his hand and wore a smile that was far too eager, too carefully arranged to be genuine. Dickinson looked brittle, his jaw set with purpose. McNairy said nothing, content to remain in the background, watching Jackson with an expression that was polite but ice-cold.

It was no secret that Jackson viewed John McNairy as a mentor, but Nathaniel had never shared that affection; he had no intention of offering the General so much as a greeting. John Overton stepped forward to bridge the gap, shaking Nathaniel's hand. "It's good to see you," he said warmly. "I just saw your brother a few days ago."

Nathaniel offered a thin, polite smile, nothing more, and stepped back into the shadow of the group.

Erwin approached then, with Dickinson flanking him like a bodyguard. His friendliness was laid on thick, a desperate coat of varnish over a cracked surface. "Gentlemen, it's always good to see you. Thomas, it has been some time. I trust you are well?"

He shook hands with each man in turn, though Charles Dickinson stood slightly apart, awkward and stiff. "This is my son-in-law, Charles," Erwin introduced.

Charles shook hands all around, his grip tight. "Congratulations on the wedding," John Overton said.

"Yes, congratulations are in order," Jackson added, his voice smooth. "Jane is a lovely young lady. Are you going to live in Nashville?"

"Yes," Charles replied. "I studied law in Maryland, but it seems there are more opportunities here in the West."

"More and more people are moving here every day," Thomas Overton noted. "A bright, ambitious young man like you will do very well."

"I'm hoping, sir."

Jackson turned back to John Overton and held out his hand. Without a word, John reached into his coat and produced a heavy envelope. Jackson took it, his fingers tapping the paper, before he looked back at Erwin. "Are we ready to proceed? I didn't see Ploughboy in the stables this morning."

Erwin's nervous smile wavered. "Andrew, I've known you a long time."

No one spoke. The Overtons and Jackson simply stared, waiting. Erwin rocked on his heels, the silence stretching until it became painful. "You see… Ploughboy… he has an infection."

"Oh," Jackson said, the syllable flat and unforgiving.

"I can't run him."

A heavy silence spread between them. Erwin tried to force his charm back into place, his voice climbing an octave. "Why not delay the race a month and allow my horse time to heal? I'll add two hundred more to the wager."

Erwin extended his hand to seal the new deal. Jackson didn't move. He rubbed his chin, his eyes fixed on Erwin's hanging hand.

"Are we in agreement?" Erwin asked, his arm still outstretched in the air.

Jackson let him hang there for a moment. "Joe, I have always held you to be a gentleman," he said at last. "You are a gentleman, are you not?"

Erwin's nod was slow and pained. He lowered his hand to his side.

"I had Judge Overton draw up a new deed," Jackson continued, his voice taking on a conversational, almost pleasant tone that felt dangerous. "He even went through the trouble to clarify that your name was spelled correctly, just as you instructed." Jackson grinned, but his eyes were like flint. "Judge Overton isn't an attorney, and he asks nothing for his time, but if a man of his ability were to draw up a deed, what would it be worth?"

"Uh, ten, twenty dollars," Erwin stammered.

"I should think it nearer thirty," Jackson replied. "But I may be mistaken. I would ask him myself, though we both know John is too modest to give an answer."

John Overton shifted, clearly uncomfortable being used as a conversational bludgeon.

"Such a man's time carries value, does it not?" Jackson asked. Erwin ground his teeth as Jackson pressed the point, while Dickinson stood by seething, his face turning a dark shade of red. Nearby, Swann and McNairy watched the spectacle, Swann with open eagerness, McNairy with a quiet, calculating intensity.

"I have fulfilled my obligations today," Jackson said, his voice hardening. "I had other matters that required my attention this morning, yet I came here with Truxton and the deed you requested. I am a man of my word, Joe. Tell me—are you?"

Erwin looked around at the gathered witnesses, then drew a deep, shaky breath. "Yes, General. I am."

"Good."

Erwin pulled a handful of bank notes from his pocket. "This is three hundred. I will get you the rest in a few weeks."

"A few weeks?" Jackson asked, counting the notes with agonizing slowness.

"Yes. I don't have access to all of it. I could get you a promissory note next week if that is agreeable."

"I would agree to half in payable notes and half in promissory notes," Jackson said, his tone shifting back to one of mock-reasonableness. "I do not wish to be unreasonable." He turned to John Overton. "Aren't we meeting Thursday after court adjourns?"

Overton nodded.

"I shall be at the City Hotel on Thursday, about four o'clock. Might you call on me that evening?"

"Yes," Erwin said, his voice barely a murmur. "I will see to it that you have the notes as agreed."

"Thank you, Joe," Jackson said, patting the envelope of money. "You are a gentleman and a man of your word."

Erwin tried to smile, but the muscles in his face refused to cooperate. Jackson shook hands with Erwin and Dickinson, then turned just enough to acknowledge McNairy with a brief, polite smile. No handshake was offered. He didn't look at Swann at all, treating the man as if he were invisible.

Jackson walked off, laughing with the Overtons, leaving the others standing in the dust of the track. Dickinson watched his back, his fists clenched. "Pompous as a peacock," he snapped. "And no gentleman."

Erwin kept his eyes fixed on Jackson's retreating form. "Quite the rascal," he muttered.

Swann and McNairy said nothing. They only watched as the noise and the dust of Clover Bottom swallowed Jackson whole, leaving them in the cold wake of his victory.

"A Damn Equivocator"

On Thursday morning, Joseph Erwin entered the parlor of Peach Bottom with irritation clinging to him like a bad smell. He stopped short at the sight of Charles Dickinson. His son-in-law was seated near the window, seemingly absorbed in a book. Dickinson didn't look up immediately; he knew his father-in-law well enough to sense that whatever storm had entered the room would announce itself soon enough.

Erwin crossed the floor with heavy strides and thrust a thick envelope into Dickinson's hands.

"Take this to the track," Erwin commanded. "Give it to the General."

Dickinson looked up, startled. He turned the envelope over in his hands as if the paper itself might explain the sudden errand. "Sir..."

"I have business to attend to," Erwin cut in sharply, already turning his back. There was a jagged edge to his tone, a dismissive quality that suggested the task was beneath him — and, by extension, beneath any further explanation.

Dickinson opened his mouth to protest, but Erwin fixed him with a look that killed the thought before it could reach his lips. The silence in the parlor grew brittle.

"I will leave now," Dickinson said at last.

He rose, tucking the envelope into the inner pocket of his coat, and exited the room without another word. Erwin remained behind, staring at the empty doorway and shaking his head in aggravated disbelief. He stood there for a long moment, looking for all the world like a man convinced the entire universe had conspired to inconvenience him personally.

♦ ♦ ♦ ♦ ♦ ♦

That night, the City Hotel in downtown Nashville was a cacophony of smoke, laughter, and the rhythmic clatter of glasses against wood. By evening, the tavern drew the city's upper ranks, lawyers, merchants, and politicians, all mixed with the ambitious men still pressing to join them. Andrew Jackson sat at the bar with the Overtons and John Coffee, commanding the center of the room without apparent effort.

Coffee, hulking and steady, sat beside him nursing a drink. A brigadier general under Jackson in the militia, he was one of the few men close enough to speak with an easy, blunt familiarity. He listened as Jackson spun a story, John Overton following along with the quiet, practiced enjoyment of a man who had heard the tale before but still found the amusement in it.

"No," Jackson was saying, his voice carrying just enough to capture the surrounding tables, "once the governor fell off his horse and broke his sword, I could tell his will to fight was also beyond repair."

The men around them roared. Jackson raised a hand, a small, magnanimous smile playing on his lips. "Now, now. I consider the matter settled. Governor Sevier is an honorable man."

The front door swung open, admitting Charles Dickinson and Thomas Swann, with Nathaniel McNairy trailing a pace behind. Dickinson spotted Jackson immediately, centered in his circle of admirers, and marched straight toward him. Swann followed with an eager, watchful gait, while McNairy casually peeled off toward the bar, remaining just far enough away to observe the coming collision without being swept up in it.

"Good evening, gentlemen," Dickinson said, clearing his throat to cut through the laughter.

The table fell silent. Coffee stood, his massive frame momentarily blocking the light. "Sir. I'm John Coffee."

Dickinson nodded and shook his hand with clipped politeness. Seeing an opening, Swann confidently thrust his own hand forward. "Good evening, John…"

Coffee flashed a thin, insincere smile, then simply took his seat again. He left Swann standing there, hand outstretched and empty—awkward, exposed, and ignored.

Dickinson turned to Overton, mindful of the judge's influence. "Judge Overton, it's a pleasure to see you. Long day at court?"

"No, no," Overton replied mildly. "It wasn't bad at all. Just some property disputes."

Dickinson finally turned his full attention to Jackson. "General, I have something for you." He produced the envelope and handed it over. Jackson took it with a nod, opened it, and began counting the contents with slow, deliberate precision.

"Four hundred from the Bank of Tennessee and a promissory note for four hundred more," Jackson announced. "Just as agreed. Thank you." He looked up, his expression unreadable. "Would you like to have a drink with us?"

Swann immediately grabbed the back of an empty

chair, his face brightening. But Dickinson didn't even look at him. "No, sir. I have to get back home. We just found out Jane is with child. She isn't feeling well."

"I suppose we'll have a drink in your honor then!" Jackson said, his tone jovial but distant.

Swann, unable to help himself, snatched a stray glass from the table. "I'll drink to that!"

Jackson ignored him entirely, his eyes fixed on Dickinson. Coffee, however, did not. "Put that down, Thomas," he snapped.

As Swann stood there, hands fumbling for a place to settle, Nathaniel McNairy drifted up beside him. He had returned from the bar with a fresh glass, a faint, mocking curl at the corner of his mouth. "Charming," McNairy murmured. The word was soft, but it hit the table like a stone in a quiet pond. "Mr. Coffee, ever the gentleman..."

Coffee's head snapped toward him, his eyes narrowing into slits. McNairy didn't blink; he simply took a slow, leisurely sip of his drink. For a moment, the air in the tavern grew dangerously thin. Jackson's gaze moved over the group, measuring the weight of the moment, before he finally lifted his glass in a silent toast.

Coffee drank. Overton clapped Dickinson on the back with forced cheer. "Thank you, gentlemen," Dickinson said, a polite smile vanishing from his face the moment he turned to leave.

Swann hurried after him, and McNairy followed a step behind, watching Coffee over the rim of his glass until they disappeared into the crowd. At the door, Swann paused to look back at the table. The laughter was already rolling on without him, the gap they had left filled instantly by the noise of the room.

As they stepped out into the night, Jackson pulled the promissory note back out of the envelope, holding it up so the lamplight caught the paper.

"General," a patron called out from across the bar, "are you buying drinks tonight?"

Jackson laughed, his voice ringing out. "I'm afraid not this evening. But once Joseph Erwin pays what he owes, I'll return and stand a round for the house!"

The patron leaned closer to Coffee. "I thought Mr. Erwin a man of means. How does he now say he cannot pay the General?"

Coffee shrugged, his voice a low rumble. "He doesn't have it. Said he just needs a little time."

The words moved like a spark through dry grass. The patron turned and whispered to the man beside him. Eyebrows shot up; heads leaned together. Voices dropped into a low, feverish hum. By the time Jackson had folded the notes and slid them back into his coat, half the bar was murmuring about Joseph Erwin's "sudden" financial ruin.

Jackson sat back, satisfied. The seeds of the rumor were planted, and in Nashville, rumors grew faster than cotton.

♦ ♦ ♦ ♦ ♦ ♦

A month later, the morning light spilled in long, dusty shafts across the stables at Clover Bottom. The air was thick with the familiar, grounding scents of sweet hay, oiled leather, and horses already worked into a lather. Joseph Erwin walked the row with Charles Dickinson, their boots thudding rhythmically against the dirt as they stopped occasionally to inspect the stock.

In a nearby stall, Redmond Barry, wealthy, genial, and perpetually comfortable in his own skin, was rhythmically brushing down his prized stallion. Erwin spotted him and changed course instantly, drawing Dickinson along in his wake like a ship pulling a tender.

"Dr. Barry, my old friend!" Erwin called out.

The men shook hands with the easy familiarity of their station. Erwin reached out to run a hand along the stallion's neck, a bright, performative smile fixed on his face. "Raging Red is a fine horse, Redmond. I recall he beat my Jolly Jim in two straight heats the last time we met."

"Indeed," Barry replied easily, not pausing his rhythm with the brush. "Red has made me a good deal of money every time I bring him to the track."

"I'd love to run Jolly Jim against him again," Erwin said, his tone casual but his eyes pressing. "But I don't have him with me today. I do have Leviathan, however. He's done quite well lately, especially at Mr. Hart's track. What do you say to a race?"

Barry's hand slowed. He smiled politely, but a flicker of discomfort crossed his face. He had no interest in racing that day, and even less in the social entanglement Erwin was offering. "Joe, Red is already set to go against one of Cannon's horses today."

"Oh," Erwin said, waving the objection away as if

it were a bothersome fly. "We can have our contest after you've embarrassed Cannon and relieved him of his notes."

"No," Barry said, his voice firming even as he maintained his cordiality. "I have other matters to attend to. Another time, perhaps."

Erwin leaned in, his voice dropping to a conspiratorial, insistent hum. "How about one hundred dollars? I'm very confident in Leviathan, Redmond. It seems to me your faith in Red is starting to waver."

The smile finally faded from Barry's face. He stopped brushing and turned fully to face his old friend. He hesitated for a heartbeat, then decided on the blunt truth. "Joe, I'll speak plainly. I believe you to be an honorable man, but there is talk at the track—whispers that you have... difficulty meeting your debts."

The words landed with the force of a physical blow. Erwin stiffened, a flash of raw offense crossing his face before he could pull the mask of the aristocrat back into place. "I am an honorable man," he muttered, the defense sounding more like a private prayer than a public statement.

But if Erwin was stunned, Dickinson was electric. He exploded forward, closing the distance between himself and Barry until they were nearly chest-to-chest.

"Sir!" Dickinson snapped, his voice cutting through the quiet of the stable like a whip. "Joe is one of the wealthiest men in Nashville. His holdings include newspapers and plantations from here to Louisiana! Do you truly believe this man cannot pay his debts?"

Erwin reached out, his fingers digging into Dickinson's arm to restrain him. "Charles, please."

Barry didn't flinch. He held his ground, his

expression resolute despite the tension. "Gentlemen, I have no doubt you are men of means. I only tell you what I heard… that you lost a considerable sum to General Jackson and were unable to pay him."

Erwin's eyes turned to flint. The "genial friend" was gone, replaced by a man cornered by his own reputation.

"I can assure you I have paid my debt to the General," he said, his voice ice-cold. "You mustn't believe everything you hear at the racetrack, Doctor. Good day."

Erwin turned sharply and stormed toward the carriages. Dickinson lingered a moment longer, his chest heaving as he glared at Barry with undisguised contempt. He waited until the silence became unbearable before turning to follow his father-in-law into the bright, unforgiving morning light.

♦♦♦♦♦♦

Later that evening, Winn's Tavern was a thick soup of tobacco smoke and frantic conversation. Charles Dickinson and a visibly irritated Joseph Erwin stepped inside, their arrival drawing a ripple of attention that Erwin clearly detested. At the bar, Thomas Swann was deep in talk with Nathaniel McNairy, but he peeled away the moment he saw them, intercepting the pair just as they claimed a table.

"Charles! Mr. Erwin… how are you, sir?" Swann's voice was eager, pitched a note too high and far too bright for the grim atmosphere.

Erwin grumbled something unintelligible, his eyes

flicking toward the bar. He could feel the weight of the room on him, curiosity sharpened into a blade by the morning's rumors.

"Thomas," Dickinson said, his voice clipped and even. "Please get us some drinks."

Relieved to have a purpose, Swann sprang into motion. A moment later, Nathaniel McNairy approached the table with an easy, feline confidence. He pulled out a chair as if it had been reserved for him since the tavern opened. "May I?"

Erwin bristled, a flash of pure irritation crossing his face, but he gave a reluctant wave of his hand. "Yes, Nathaniel. Please."

McNairy settled in smoothly, looking like a man who was exactly where he intended to be. Once Swann was out of earshot, Erwin leaned forward, his voice a low, gravelly hiss. "Andrew Jackson. That backhanded yokel. Can't keep his damn mouth shut."

McNairy took the vitriol in without comment, his eyes moving quietly from face to face, measuring the temperature of the table.

"And for that, he'll pay a price," Dickinson added, his jaw set.

Swann returned, setting Erwin's glass down with exaggerated care before taking a seat. Sensing the lethal tension, he tried to pivot to safer ground. "Um, Mr. Erwin, I just wanted to congratulate you. I understand you'll soon become a grandfather."

Erwin waved him off as if dismissing a servant. "Yes, yes…"

Swann glanced at Dickinson, visibly confused by the cold indifference. "It's the General," Dickinson explained quietly. "He's been telling everyone in

Nashville that Joe cannot pay his debts."

Swann seized the opening, playing the part of the indignant messenger. He gestured vaguely toward the barkeep. "When I came in here, Mr. Winn himself asked about your… uh… financial difficulties."

The blood rushed to Erwin's face. At the bar, the bartender suddenly found a glass that needed intense polishing. Several men turned their backs, pretending to be deeply interested in their own drinks, though their ears were tilted toward the table.

"Difficulties?" Erwin snapped.

"I told them you satisfactorily settled the debt!" Swann said quickly, his voice rising. "I watched Charles hand him the notes myself." McNairy gave a single, deliberate nod—a silent reinforcement that carried more weight than Swann's chatter.

Suddenly, Erwin shot to his feet. He glared toward the crowded bar, his voice booming over the din. "Did you hear that? I satisfied my debt to General Jackson!"

The tavern went dead. Conversations stalled mid-sentence; even Mr. Winn paused with a bottle tilted over a glass. Dickinson lunged upward, grabbing Erwin by the arm and hauling him back into his chair. The room let out a slow, collective exhale, but the silence remained brittle.

Erwin wasn't finished. He slammed his fist onto the table, sending the glasses rattling. "His mother was a whore," he spat, the words pouring out of him like venom. "His father was a mulatto." He turned his head and looked straight at McNairy, his voice rising again. "Had he not ridden your brother's favor into town, he'd be nothing more than a clerk in a general store! The man lives in bigamy, yet he struts about Nashville as if he were its king!"

Dickinson stood again, his eyes dark. "Leave this to me, Joe. I'll find him."

"You will not!" Erwin barked. "Sit down!"

Dickinson obeyed, though his chair shrieked against the floorboards.

"I expect to see him at the City Hotel this evening," Swann offered tentatively. "He always calls on Judge Overton after court."

"Tell him he's a damn equivocator," Dickinson snapped at Swann, "and it would serve him best to stop spreading such falsehoods."

"Now, now," Erwin said, his rage settling into a cold, hard simmer. He lifted his glass. "He'll be at the track this weekend. I may be old, but I can still fight my own battles."

Dickinson leaned toward Swann, his voice a lethal whisper. "I'll go with you."

Erwin drained his whiskey in one swallow and slammed the empty glass down so hard it nearly shattered. "Another!" he shouted toward the bar.

Heads turned again, and a few men exchanged knowing, worried looks. Swann jumped to his feet, eager to escape the heat of the table. "Right away, sir."

McNairy sat back, watching the wreckage. He couldn't help himself—a brief, sharp chuckle escaped him before he quickly stifled it behind his hand.

A few hours later, the City Hotel was a fever of noise and lamplight, the air a stagnant fog of tobacco smoke and laughter. Andrew Jackson stepped inside, his cane tapping a rhythmic, authoritative beat against the floorboards. He paused to scan the room as he always did, measuring faces, weighing the tilt of a chin, noting who met his gaze and who suddenly found their drink fascinating.

At a nearby table sat the Benton brothers. Thomas, a young attorney, sat with a refined, polished composure that suggested a man careful of his future. Beside him, Jesse practiced a different sort of law — the kind found in the bottom of a bottle and the heat of a tavern brawl. He looked entirely entertained by the surrounding chaos.

As Jackson passed, the brothers exchanged a sharp glance. "Thomas, better hide your wife," Jesse muttered. It was low, but in the sudden lull of the room, it carried like a shot.

They snickered. Jackson's head snapped around, his eyes locking onto Thomas Benton with the intensity of a predator. The humor evaporated from their table instantly. Both brothers straightened, their spines hitting the backs of their chairs.

"Mr. Benton," Jackson said, his voice a low vibration.

Thomas tipped his hat. It was a gesture just respectful enough to keep the peace, though only barely. Jesse struggled to swallow a lingering grin. Jackson moved on, a visible irritation simmering just beneath the surface of his skin.

He spotted the Overton brothers and pulled up a chair. A barkeep, sensing the General's mood, hurried over to set down a round of drinks before a word was even spoken.

"Andrew," John said, his eyes drifting toward the far side of the room. Jackson followed his gaze to the Bentons. His jaw tensed until the muscles bunched.

"Those damn Benton boys," he muttered.

Across the room, Jesse Benton noticed the attention and let out a small, high-pitched giggle. Thomas raised his glass in a mock salute, offering John a deliberate, slow wink. John returned a restrained, judicial nod, while Thomas Overton dropped his eyes, suddenly gripped by a fascination with the amber liquid in his glass.

The front door opened, Charles Dickinson, Thomas Swann, and Nathaniel McNairy entered. Dickinson looked coiled, his every movement intentional. Swann, however, looked transformed—his shoulders were back, his chest out, buoyed by the presence of men who actually carried weight in the town. McNairy followed at a languid distance, his eyes already fixed on Jackson. He wasn't looking for a fight; he was looking for a show.

At the Overtons' table, the conversation continued as if no one else existed. "Did you ever sell that property on the Gallatin square?" Thomas Overton asked.

"I'm going up there next week," Jackson replied. "I have yet to sign the papers."

The newcomers took seats at the very next table, close enough to breathe the same air, close enough to force a confrontation.

"Excuse me, gentlemen," Swann said.

The Overtons glanced over, but Jackson remained a statue. He turned his shoulder slightly, dismissing Swann with a silence that was louder than a shout.

"Did they send us a contract?" Jackson asked John.

"Yes, there are some…"

"Gentlemen," Swann pressed, leaning into their space.

Jackson's restraint was a wire pulled to the breaking point. John Overton saw the danger and tried to intercept it. "Thomas, we are…"

"Sir, I wanted…" Swann cut in, his voice emboldened by his companions.

Jackson turned fully then. His voice was level, but it held the cold, flat resonance of a tombstone. "Why do you see fit to interject yourself when it is clear to everyone here that we are having a private conversation?"

Thomas Overton's breath hitched. He had seen the General angry, but this was something else — the precise instant where the man's iron control simply ceased to exist.

With Dickinson and McNairy at his shoulder, Swann found a swagger he had never earned. "Sir, you speak of this man's family…"

Jackson was airborne before the sentence could finish. His chair screeched backward, hitting the floor with a crash. He seized the heavy cane leaning against the table and swung it in a vicious, horizontal arc. It connected with the side of Swann's head with a sound like a wet branch snapping.

Swann went down hard.

For a heartbeat, the tavern froze. Dickinson and McNairy stood paralyzed, their minds unable to process how quickly the social posturing had turned to blood. Then the room erupted. Jackson struck again, and then a third time, his rage finally unbound and howling.

The Overtons lunged at him, grabbing his arms, fighting the wiry strength of a man possessed. Thomas

Benton leapt from his chair and dropped to the floor beside Swann, where blood was already spreading in a dark, widening pool.

"Thomas! Thomas!" Dickinson shouted, his voice cracking as he collapsed beside the fallen man.

McNairy finally found his voice. "Blazes, Andrew," he gasped. "What are you doing?"

Jackson spun on him, his eyes blazing with a terrifying, pale light. He snarled, a sound more animal than human, and wrenched himself free of the Overtons' grip. The cane lowered slowly, the tip red, but his eyes remained pinned to McNairy's throat.

The room held its breath. The violence was still there, coiled and waiting in the center of the room, daring anyone to draw a long breath.

"He needs a doctor!" Thomas Benton shouted, his hands pressed to Swann's head.

John Overton grabbed McNairy by the arm before the young man could take a step toward the General. "If you wish to fight," McNairy barked, struggling against the Judge, "put that weapon away!"

Jackson ground his teeth, his chest heaving with the exertion of his fury. Thomas Overton rushed to help his brother, and together they shoved McNairy toward the door, dragging him out into the night. The tavern slowly exhaled, the immediate danger retreating, but the air remained thick with the scent of blood and sweat.

Jesse Benton sauntered over at his own pace, hands deep in his pockets, whistling a soft, tuneless melody as he surveyed the wreckage. He looked down at Swann's shattered face and shook his head with a flicker of genuine amusement.

"My," he said lightly, the words cutting through

the silence. "The General very nearly killed him."

Swann writhed on the floor, a low, animal moan escaping his throat. With Thomas Benton's help, he was hauled upright, blood covering his face and his nose pushed into an ugly, crooked angle. He sagged against Benton, his eyes vacant and dazed.

Jackson didn't watch them leave. He turned his back on the carnage, sat down, and adjusted his chair so he faced the bar. With a hand that was perfectly steady, he took a slow, deliberate sip of his glass.

The tavern didn't return to its roar. It stayed hushed. Men leaned back, avoiding eye contact. Whispers moved through the shadows in nervous, shivering waves.

Swann tried to take a step, his legs buckled, and he collapsed again. Thomas Benton caught him and eased him down, staying close. Dickinson straightened, his fists clenched so tight his knuckles were white as bone, and followed them toward the exit.

All around them, the tavern buzzed — voices overlapping, chairs scraping, men leaning in for a better look. By morning, every detail would be exaggerated, repeated, and sharpened, but the damage had already been done.

Satisfaction

The four of them, Dickinson, McNairy, and the Benton brothers—half-carried Thomas Swann through the Nashville night. He hung heavy between them, stumbling as blood streaked his face and poured into the front of his shirt.

"There," Thomas Benton said, pointing toward a modest house ahead. He stepped forward and struck the door with a sharp, insistent knock.

A few seconds later, the door creaked open to reveal an older man, bald and squinting against the darkness in his bedclothes. "Yes?" he asked, his voice thick with sleep.

"Dr. White," Thomas said, "this man needs your attention."

White took in the bloody scene, opened the door wider, and stepped aside. "Bring him in. What happened?"

Before anyone else could find their voice, McNairy spoke up, his tone flat and accusatory. "Andrew Jackson beat him. Plain enough."

White said nothing. He ushered them into a small, lamp-lit room where Swann was guided into a chair. The young man collapsed into the seat, his head lolling. White dropped to one knee in front of him, studying the wreckage of his face with the detached, practiced eye of a man who had seen the frontier's worst.

"It appears his nose is broken," the doctor said calmly.

He fetched a length of clean cloth and began wrapping it around Swann's head, tightening the bandage with careful, firm hands. "This should slow the bleeding." He paused, his hands hovering, as he looked Swann squarely in the eye. "This may hurt, son."

Without further warning, White took Swann's nose firmly between his thumb and forefinger and shoved the bone back into place.

Jesse Benton winced, the sound of the cartilage snapping making his own stomach turn. Swann didn't just moan; he screamed — a raw, high-pitched sound that echoed off the medicinal cabinets.

White leaned back, seemingly satisfied. "Rest is the best medicine now. Give him time. His wounds will heal."

"Is there anything else that must be done?" Dickinson asked, his voice tight with a mixture of pity and burgeoning rage.

White shook his head, wiping his hands on a towel. "Not tonight."

McNairy turned to Dickinson, his expression hardening into something cold and permanent. "There is more still to be done."

He glanced at the doctor. "Doctor, may I trouble you for a sheet of paper?"

White crossed to a cabinet and retrieved a sheet. The Bentons watched silently as he handed it over. Dickinson leaned in closer as McNairy began to write, the scratch of the quill sounding louder than it should have in the quiet room.

A few moments later, Thomas Benton pushed back through the doors of the City Hotel, a folded sheet of paper in his hand. He paused just inside, then scanned the room. It didn't take long to find who he was looking for — Andrew Jackson, seated at his usual table with John Overton and Thomas Overton, and John Coffee, who had joined them only moments before.

Benton crossed the room.

Jackson looked up as he approached, curiosity crossing his face.

Benton glanced at Coffee and gave a short, crooked smile. "Hello, John. It appears you missed the excitement earlier." He let out a quiet chuckle at his own understatement.

Every man at the table straightened, alert now. Benton shifted his weight, then turned fully to Jackson.

"General… this is for you."

Jackson took the letter. Benton remained standing.

Jackson unfolded the paper and read in silence.

General Jackson,
Sir,
Tonight, in full view of respectable company, you saw fit to assault my friend Thomas Swann with a cane, armed violence visited upon an unarmed man whose only offense was the wish to share a drink and speak his mind. Such conduct may pass among rough men, but it cannot be excused among gentlemen.

To strike a man with a weapon while he stands defenseless is not bravery. It is the act of a bully, one who relies on force where honor fails him.

If you believe your actions were those of a man of courage, you will have no difficulty answering for them. I therefore demand satisfaction for the insult done to my friend and to myself as witness to it. I stand ready to meet you in the customary manner, at such time and place as may be agreed upon, each man standing equal and armed with a pistol.

Should you decline this challenge, the world will judge whether your valor extends beyond the reach of a cane.

I await your reply.

Your obedient servant,
N. McNairy

Jackson lowered the letter and set it carefully on the scarred wood of the table. Both Overtons leaned in at once, their necks craning to scan the jagged script on the page. John Coffee, however, leaned back. He ignored the paper, choosing instead to read the man, watching Jackson's face for the slight tightening of the jaw that signaled a coming storm.

Jackson sat in a heavy, contemplative silence as the dull roar of the tavern washed around them.

"He is beneath you," John Overton said, his voice low and urgent. "Do not respond."

"What is his trouble with you, Andrew?" Thomas Overton asked.

Jackson exhaled, a long, weary sound. "His brother took an interest in me. Helped me greatly when I was a young man. Perhaps Nathaniel feels slighted that John didn't go to greater lengths to advance his own career. He has always been disagreeable toward me."

John Overton leaned further over the table, his tone sharpening. "He is beneath you, Andrew. You must not respond."

At the edge of the circle, Thomas Benton absorbed every word, his expression an unreadable mask.

"I want to put a ball straight through him," Jackson said quietly. He paused, then shook his head. "But I will not fight young McNairy."

Suddenly, Coffee stood. His chair screeched across the floorboards like a warning. He fixed Benton with a hard, towering stare that made the younger man swallow hard. "He wants a challenge?" Coffee rumbled. "Where is he?"

Coffee was a mountain of a man, broad, solid, and radiating a quiet, military violence. Benton didn't want any trouble. "Uh, he told me to meet him at Winn's Tavern," Benton stammered. "With the General's decision."

Coffee was already moving toward the door. "Let's go."

"John…" Jackson called out, his voice sharp with warning. Thomas Overton half-rose, his hand instinctively reaching out to catch Coffee's sleeve, but he thought better of it and let his hand fall limp.

Benton turned and led the way into the night, with Coffee trailing behind him like a dark omen. They marched down the street and straight into the belly of Winn's Tavern.

Inside, the air was thick with the scent of cheap whiskey and tobacco. Charles Dickinson sat at a table with Nathaniel McNairy, their heads together in mid-conversation, glasses in hand. McNairy's back was to the door; he never saw the shadow fall across the table.

Coffee crossed the room with terrifying speed. Before a word could be uttered, he yanked a loaded whip from his belt and swung it in a vicious, blind-side arc. The weighted lash caught McNairy high on the head, snapping his neck sideways. McNairy went down in a chaotic tangle of splintering chair legs and spilled drink.

Coffee was on him in an instant. He brought the whip down again and again, the leather cracking through the din of the tavern like pistol shots. McNairy curled into a ball on the floor, his arms thrown up to shield his head as the blows landed with sickening thuds.

"Stop!" Dickinson leapt up, shouting for help. The Benton brothers rushed in, and together the three of them threw themselves at Coffee, dragging the big man backward with brute effort. Chairs skidded and overturned as they wrestled him away from the bloody heap on the floor.

The whip slipped from Coffee's hand and clattered onto the floorboards. McNairy staggered to his feet, blood leaking from his mouth. He spotted the weapon, lunged for it, and seized it.

With a violent, shoulder-rolling shrug, Coffee shook free of his captors. McNairy didn't hesitate. He swung.

The whip cracked across Coffee's face—hard, clean, and devastating. Coffee's head snapped back, light bursting behind his eyes as the room tilted dangerously. He staggered, his hand flying instinctively to his mouth.

Thomas Benton lunged between them, his arms spread wide like a barrier. "Enough!" he bellowed.

The tavern froze. Behind the bar, Mr. Winn's voice boomed over the wreckage. "No fighting! Not in here!"

The warning hung in the air, heavy and final. Every man in the room understood how close the night had come to total bloodshed.

Coffee straightened slowly. His jaw worked as he tested the hinge of it, a white-hot pain radiating up into his skull. He spat a thick, red glob and something small and white clattered onto the tavern floor.

A tooth.

The room went dead quiet. Coffee stared down at the ivory fragment for a heartbeat, then looked back at McNairy. Whatever restraint had lived there a moment earlier was gone, replaced by something cold, predatory, and far more dangerous. His chest heaved, his breath dragging.

"Mr. Coffee, please," Thomas Benton whispered, the urgency in his voice turning to genuine fear.

Coffee's hand slipped into the inner pocket of his coat. McNairy froze. Coffee's fingers closed around the cold grip of a pistol. He drew it just enough, just an inch of steel, for McNairy to see it, to understand exactly what waited on the other side of another mistake.

For a long, agonizing moment, the tavern held its breath. Then, Coffee exhaled through his nose. Slowly, deliberately, he let the pistol slide back inside his coat. He took one step backward, then another, his eyes never leaving McNairy's.

The silence held as Coffee turned and pushed through the door. Outside, he stepped into the cool night air, rubbing his throbbing jaw and cursing under his breath. He stopped beneath the tavern's front window and caught his reflection in the glass.

Blood streaked his chin. His lip was split, and when he bared his teeth in disbelief, a dark, jagged gap stared back at him. He wiped his mouth with the back of his hand, leaving a crimson smear on his sleeve. He stared at the stranger in the glass for a moment longer, breathing hard, then turned and vanished into the dark. Each footstep was a promise that this was not a conclusion, only a postponement.

♦ ♦ ♦ ♦ ♦ ♦

The following night, the City Hotel was a different place. The crowd was thinner, the roar of the previous evening replaced by a heavy, expectant mood. Andrew Jackson sat at a corner table with John Overton and James Robertson. Robertson, the distinguished founder of Nashville, sat with a calm, weathered presence that commanded immediate respect. They were deep in conversation when John Coffee entered, his eyes scanning the room with a cold efficiency before he pulled up a chair.

Jackson looked up at once. His gaze flicked immediately to Coffee's mouth — the dark, jagged gap where the tooth had been and the swelling bruise that carved a path along his jaw.

"I heard about your fight with Nathaniel," Jackson said, his voice low.

"I just met with Jesse Benton," Coffee replied, his tone as even as a soldier's report. "He demands satisfaction… from me."

Robertson's attention sharpened at the word. The air at the table grew still.

"I will give it to him," Coffee continued, his eyes locked on Jackson. "I have business in Knoxville first. But when I return, I mean to meet McNairy on the first of March."

Jackson blinked, momentarily caught off guard by the finality of the date. Overton caught Jackson's eye, giving him a sharp, warning look that shouted *don't* without a single word being spoken.

"John…" Overton began, reaching out.

"No," Coffee said, cutting him off without breaking eye contact with the General. He leaned in slightly. "Will you serve as my second?"

Jackson hesitated. The request settled between them like a physical weight, thick with the implication of what it meant to stand on a field of honor. "Very well," Jackson said at last.

Robertson leaned forward, his voice a soft, reasoned plea. "John, there is no need to pursue such a perilous course."

Coffee looked the old pioneer in the eye. "Sir…"

Robertson grimaced and held up a hand, realizing the futility of the argument. "If you insist on this, it cannot take place here. You will be arrested. Dueling is strictly forbidden by the laws of this state."

"There's a mill in Logan County, Kentucky," Jackson interjected, his mind already moving with tactical precision. "Just over the Red River."

"I am familiar with the area," Coffee said.

"I'll speak with Mr. Benton," Jackson went on, calculating the distances and the legalities. "I'll make the preparations."

Coffee gave a single, sharp nod of acknowledgment. Jackson leaned closer, his voice dropping to a near whisper. "You are certain you wish to see this affair of honor through to the end?"

Robertson tried one last time, his voice weary. "You do not have to take up arms to settle this matter."

Coffee's face remained like stone, the bruise on his jaw a dark badge of his intent. "Yes. I will meet McNairy in the field."

Robertson leaned back in his chair, watching the

two men with the resigned look of a father watching a house burn. There was nothing left to say.

"Very well." Robertson shook his head slowly and took a long, slow drink from his glass, the amber liquid offering no answers to the violence on the horizon.

Unobstructed

March 1, 1806, Logan County, Kentucky

Jackson and Coffee stood in the open field, the Red River stretching behind them like a silver ribbon, slow and indifferent beneath the pale morning light. Coffee said nothing, and he did not need to; Jackson understood the silence. He glanced once at his friend, then turned his gaze to the water, letting the heavy minutes pass without comment.

A carriage appeared in the distance, its dark shape rising over the crest of the low road. Jackson straightened, his frame becoming a rigid line against the horizon. "Nathaniel has arrived."

Coffee lifted his head and drew a slow, deliberate breath through his nose. The carriage rolled closer, the crunch of its wheels loud in the morning quiet, before coming to a halt. Jesse Benton stepped down first, followed by Nathaniel McNairy. McNairy's expression was carefully composed, a mask of aristocratic calm that didn't quite hide the tension in his shoulders.

They looked across the field, spotting Jackson and Coffee waiting like statues. McNairy leaned toward Jesse, their heads close as they spoke quietly. After a moment, McNairy reached into his coat and drew out his pistol, the steel glinting in the early light.

Jesse gestured toward the center of the field and stepped forward. Jackson broke away from Coffee to meet him halfway.

"Does he wish to delope?" Jesse asked, referring to the practice of firing into the air to satisfy honor without blood.

Jackson glanced back at his friend. Coffee was inspecting his own pistol with a practiced, terrifying calm. "No," Jackson said flatly. "He means to fire."

"That was my expectation," Jesse replied. "Nathaniel proposes thirty paces."

"We will count down from five," Jackson countered. "Pistols at the side. On the word, raise and fire."

Jesse studied the General, searching for a tremor that wasn't there. "Do you wish to count, or shall I?"

Jackson held his gaze, measuring the younger Benton. "You may do it, Jesse, if you wish."

Jackson returned to Coffee. "Thirty paces," he said quietly. "Jesse will count from five. Then fire."

Coffee didn't answer; he only checked his flintlock one last time. Jackson rested a hand on the big man's shoulder, his voice dropping to a whisper. "If you wish to delope and walk away, I can speak to Jesse. It is not too late, John."

Coffee drew a deep breath and shook his head. The decision was made.

They walked further into the field until they reached the center. Jesse began counting out the distance, his boots thumping against the sod. Thirty paces out, he dropped a stone to mark the mark.

"General." Jesse pointed to the ground.

Coffee stopped and turned back to Jackson. They held each other's eyes for a heartbeat longer than necessary — a silent acknowledgment that this might be the last time they looked upon one another. The thought cut deep into Jackson, but he kept his face a mask of iron.

Coffee walked to his mark. Jesse looked to

McNairy, who gave a sharp nod. He looked to Coffee, who returned the gesture.

"Five," Jesse called out. Coffee's finger twitched against the trigger guard.

"Four." McNairy's breathing became audible, heavy and ragged.

"Three." Jackson drew a slow breath, his heart hammering against his ribs. He wanted to look away, but he couldn't.

"Two…"

BANG.

The premature crack of McNairy's pistol split the morning. A second blast followed almost instantly — the accidental discharge of a falling man. Jackson's eyes widened as Coffee cried out and collapsed, clutching his right thigh. The pain tore a raw scream from his throat as he hit the ground. His own ball had driven straight into the dirt at his feet.

Smoke hung low and acrid in the still air. Jackson and Jesse rushed to the fallen man. Jackson looked up, fury flooding his face as he locked onto McNairy. "What have you done?"

McNairy stood frozen, staring at the smoking weapon in his hand as if it were a poisonous serpent. He looked unable to believe he had fired so soon or that he had broken the most sacred rule of the field.

Coffee lay in the grass, his breath coming in sharp, ragged bursts of profanity. He pressed a hand to the wound, but blood spilled freely through his fingers, staining the earth. He gritted his teeth and looked up at Jackson. "Help me up."

Jackson slipped an arm under him and hauled him upright. Nathaniel rushed forward, his face as pale as a shroud. "I'm… I'm terribly sorry," he stammered, the words tumbling over each other. "I didn't mean…"

Jackson ignored the apology. He held Coffee steady and turned his head toward Jesse. "Send him back to his mark."

Jesse hesitated, his eyes wide. "General…"

"He has yet to fire," Jackson said, his voice as cold as the river. "Unobstructed. Thirty paces. Nathaniel will place his pistol on the ground."

McNairy's eyes widened in pure horror. He knew the code. Since he had fired early, Coffee or his second, now had the right to take a deliberate, aimed shot at a defenseless man.

Jesse looked at his friend, then back at Jackson. "The General is correct."

"Nathaniel," Jackson said, his voice a lethal monotone. "Go to your mark. Your pistol, place it on the ground."

McNairy's shoulders sagged. He walked back to his mark like a man heading to the gallows and set his pistol in the grass. He stood there empty-handed, shivering and defeated.

Jackson looked at Coffee. "Do you wish to fire?"

Coffee glanced at his leg, the trousers soaked through with crimson. He grimaced and shook his head. "I am not certain I am able."

Jesse looked to Jackson. "You may answer for him."

Jackson's eyes slid back to McNairy. The young man couldn't stand still; his weight shifted from foot to foot, fear written in every line of his body. Jackson looked back at his wounded friend. He did not want to kill his mentor's brother, but the laws of honor demanded a price.

"John," Jackson said quietly, "what would you have me do?"

Coffee paused, his gaze drifting over to the shivering McNairy. "General," he said, his voice tight with agony, "you could fell him."

McNairy heard the words and froze. Coffee forced a thin, pained grin. "But I have another idea."

Jackson waited.

"Let him write to the papers and say plainly what occurred," Coffee said. "Tell exactly how the shot came early."

Jackson considered the proposition. "Is that what you would have?"

Coffee smirked. "He will be known as a coward for the rest of his days. That lasts longer than a funeral."

Jesse let out a short, involuntary chuckle of disbelief. He walked over to McNairy, who began nodding frantically before Jesse could even finish the proposal.

"I will write the letter tonight!" McNairy cried, relief and shame mixing in equal measure. "I swear it. I'll set the matter straight. You have my word!"

Suddenly overly polite, McNairy babbled his well-wishes for their safe travels. Jackson said nothing. He only tightened his grip on Coffee's arm and began the slow, painful trek toward the carriage. The matter was settled, not with lead, but with a stain on McNairy's name that would never wash out.

The next day Nathaniel McNairy stood in his room quickly folding shirts into an open trunk. Boots, papers, and a few personal effects. He was reaching for a coat when a knock sounded at the door.

He froze.

After a long, brittle silence, he crossed the room and cracked the door open just an inch. Charles Dickinson stood in the hallway, flanked by Thomas Swann. Swann was a gruesome sight, still sporting two blackened eyes and a swollen, purple bridge across his nose from Jackson's cane.

McNairy exhaled a long, shaky breath through his nose. He opened the door wider and stepped aside, the unease written in every jagged line of his face.

Dickinson entered first, his eyes immediately surveying the disarray of the room before stopping on the half-packed trunk. "Nathaniel," he said, his voice flat. "What are you doing?"

"Urgent business in New Orleans," McNairy replied, his words tumbling out too fast to be entirely believed. "My uncle sent word yesterday. I must depart at once."

Dickinson didn't respond. His eyes drifted past McNairy to a small writing table in the corner. A single sheet of paper sat there, the quill still resting in the inkwell beside it. McNairy caught the look and shifted casually, placing his body between Dickinson and the table, as though by some clumsy accident.

Swann leaned against the doorframe, his battered face twisting as he crossed his arms. "Were you hurt on the field, Nathaniel?"

McNairy didn't look up. "No."

Swann's eyes narrowed, the dark bruising making

his stare even more predatory. "And what became of Mr. Coffee? Did he fall?"

McNairy's hands faltered over a silk waistcoat. He shifted his weight, his fingers nervously brushing the brass edge of the trunk. "Mr. Coffee and I…" He stopped, cleared his throat, and tried again. "We made peace on the field. There is no quarrel between us now."

Dickinson and Swann exchanged a look—brief, puzzled, and entirely unconvinced. In the world they inhabited, "peace" on a dueling ground usually meant lead or a public apology, and McNairy was far too intact for the former.

"If you'll excuse me," McNairy said, already turning his back on them to hide the shame creeping up his neck. "I must finish my packing."

Neither man pressed him further. The air in the room had turned sour with the unspoken truth. They stepped back into the hall, their skepticism trailing behind them like a shadow as the door clicked shut.

McNairy stood there for a long moment, his head bowed, listening to their footsteps fade down the corridor. Once the silence returned, he went back to the trunk and resumed packing, this time with a desperate, clawing urgency, as if he could pack away the memory of the Red River before the morning stagecoach arrived.

"A Lady in Every Respect"

January 29, 1835, Washington D.C.

President Jackson sat up in bed, laughing so hard the sound collapsed into a rough coughing fit that left him clutching his chest. Dr. Sneed stared at him, mouth hanging open, unable to reconcile the wheezing old man before him with the stories he'd just heard.

Sarah Jackson rushed in at once, alarmed. Jackson caught sight of her and waved a hand. "Go on, dear. Don't worry about me."

She exhaled slowly, searching his face, then reluctantly stepped back out of the room. Jackson turned his attention to Sneed again, a grin still tugging at his mouth. "As might be expected, Nathaniel McNairy was not seen again in Nashville for some time."

Sneed shook his head, a soft chuckle escaping him despite himself. "But the ball," he said at last, gesturing toward Jackson's chest. "The one lodged in you." Jackson glanced down, almost thoughtfully. "Oh yes."

March 3, 1806, Nashville, Tennessee

Andrew and Rachel Jackson rode side by side in their carriage, the wheels rattling softly over the street. Jackson held a newspaper open in his hands, scanning it once more before letting out a quiet, satisfied chuckle.

He tilted the paper toward Rachel. "Look here."

She leaned closer as he read aloud, the words carrying the stiff formality of public contrition:

I have ever held Mr. John Coffee in the highest esteem and have regarded him as a gentleman of unquestioned character. We met upon the dueling ground under circumstances most regrettable, and I must state plainly that I discharged my pistol by accident, before the word was given. For this impropriety I offer my sincere apology, both to Mr. Coffee and to the public, and trust that the matter may now rest.

Rachel read the paper twice, then looked up at him, a small smile forming. Jackson folded it, still visibly amused. As the carriage slowed and came to a stop, Jackson stepped down first, then turned to help his wife. Rachel followed, her movements careful and quiet, her unease plain as she took in the scene. Jackson steadied her as she descended.

"There you go, dear."

As they moved away from the carriage, Rachel lowered her voice. "I feel dreadfully out of place here, Andrew. All these scoundrels smoking cigars and drinking whiskey. It hardly seems a place for a lady."

Jackson smiled and squeezed her hand. "Nonsense. The most refined man I know will be here."

Rachel looked up at him. "Oh?"

"Myself," Jackson said with a twinkle in his eye. Rachel chuckled, shaking her head. "John will be here as well," Jackson added.

Rachel's face brightened at once, her discomfort easing. She lit up as they started toward the track together. He took up his cane and, hand in hand, they headed toward the stables. Rachel kept her eyes lowered. Halfway across the grounds, Jackson spotted Joseph Erwin and Charles Dickinson standing near the rail, watching the horses run. Swann and McNairy were noticeably absent.

"Excuse me, darling," Jackson said softly. "I'll be right back."

Rachel paused where she was, a look of curiosity on her face as Jackson released her hand and turned away. She watched from a distance as he crossed the track toward the two men. Erwin saw him coming and turned cold. Dickinson stood behind him, posture rigid, his presence meant to be felt. Jackson approached, making a visible effort to keep his tone cordial.

"Joe, I must speak with you. Matters are getting beyond control."

"Andrew," Erwin coldly replied.

"Is there a problem?" Jackson asked.

Dickinson stepped forward. Jackson's fingers tightened slightly around his cane. "What have you been saying about Joe?" Dickinson demanded.

Jackson bit down on his temper. "Young man, if you please… step back."

Dickinson held his gaze for a moment, then retreated a few steps, returning to Erwin's side.

"One of your friends refused a race," Erwin said,

"claiming he doubts my ability to pay my debts. You wouldn't happen to know the source of that notion?"

Jackson looked at him, surprised. "I know it's been difficult of late to draw large sums from the bank. I've had the same trouble for months. I would never disparage your name, Joe."

Dickinson stepped forward again. "I find that hard to accept, sir."

Jackson glared at him, then turned his attention back to Erwin. "Joe, if your son-in-law means to accuse me, let him say so outright."

Erwin cut Dickinson a sharp look. Dickinson faltered and stared down at the ground. Jackson stepped closer and rested a hand on Erwin's shoulder, the gesture familiar but deliberate—an attempt at calm amid the tension. From across the grounds, Rachel watched silently, sensing the heaviness of the moment without hearing a word.

"How long have we known one another?" Jackson asked.

Erwin hesitated, silently counting years he'd never bothered to number.

"Joe," Jackson said gently, "you're my friend. If I hear anyone speaking ill of you or anyone in your family, I assure you I will speak up on your behalf."

"Thank you," Erwin said.

"You have my word," Jackson promised. They shook hands. "I understand you're going to be a grandfather," Jackson added.

Erwin smiled.

"I'm very happy for you. Children are truly a blessing. You know… if it's a boy, Andrew is a fine name."

Erwin chuckled. "I told Jane they should name it Joseph whether it's a boy or a girl."

Jackson laughed with him. "A fine name indeed."

Dickinson remained unimpressed, arms stiff at his sides. Jackson glanced past them and caught sight of Rachel standing apart, arms crossed, watching him intently. "I must return to my wife. Please excuse me, gentlemen."

Erwin nodded, still smiling. Jackson turned to Dickinson, making one last attempt at peace. "Young man, your friend… is he faring well? I wish I had exercised more restraint in the tavern."

Dickinson refused to look him in the eye.

"I trust your new law practice will prosper," Jackson said. He patted Dickinson on the shoulder and strode back toward Rachel.

Once Jackson was gone, Dickinson spoke through clenched teeth. "You cannot believe him."

"I don't know," Erwin said. "It must be either him or one of the Overtons."

Dickinson's mouth tightened. "He arrives on cue." He motioned toward the track, where John Overton stood watching two horses thunder past. "There's the judge."

They walked over together. "Good afternoon, Judge," Erwin said.

"Joe, are you well?" Overton replied, then rubbed his chin as he searched for the younger man's name. "Forgive me, I'm poor with names."

Dickinson extended his hand and Overton shook it. "Charles, sir."

"Oh yes, of course," Overton said. "I beg your pardon. Have you set up your practice yet?"

"I've entered into a lease for an office on Cherry Street."

"That's good to hear, son," Overton said warmly. "If I can ever be of assistance, you need only call on me at the courthouse. My chambers are open to you."

"Thank you, sir."

Erwin shifted his weight, then asked carefully, "I would ask you about a matter. There is talk that I do not meet my debts. Have you heard it?"

Overton looked genuinely surprised. "I've heard nothing of it. Have you spoken with Andrew?"

"Yes," Erwin said. "He insists he knows nothing of the matter."

Overton nodded slowly as the horses raced on and the worry refused to leave Erwin's face. Jackson returned with Rachel at his side. John Overton's face softened immediately; he stepped forward and wrapped her in a warm embrace. There was an ease between them, the kind born of their time together in the boardinghouse in Harrodsburg, Kentucky years earlier. Rachel returned the hug, clearly comforted by him.

Dickinson made a point of avoiding Jackson. He shifted away and positioned himself beside Overton instead, eyes lowered, jaw tight.

"You're looking especially well, Rachel," Erwin said.

Rachel offered a shy smile. "Thank you."

"And are the races to your liking?" Erwin asked.

"Oh, it's quite delightful," Rachel said. "I'm eager to see Truxton run again. Was he not to have raced one of your horses?"

Erwin hesitated just a fraction of a second, long enough to register, but he kept his tone polite. "Yes.

Ploughboy has taken an infection and will be unfit to race for some time. I trust we may yet see the two meet on the track."

"Truxton will leave Ploughboy out of sight!" Rachel said brightly.

Jackson smiled, carefully this time. Dickinson gave a short laugh.

"Yes," Dickinson muttered to John Overton, "about as far out of sight as Mrs. Jackson left her first husband when she went off with the General."

Overton's jaw dropped. He turned slowly toward Dickinson, keeping his voice low. "That is wholly inappropriate. Rachel Jackson is a lady in every respect."

Dickinson dismissed him with a shrug and walked away. Rachel, unaware, pointed toward a white horse that had just stumbled across the finish well behind the rest. "My, my," she said. "That one runs a race exactly as a Federalist."

A few men chuckled.

"She speaks the truth," Jackson said. "Look around, no one stands with him."

Laughter broke out across the group, everyone doubling over except John Overton. He managed a smile, but his eyes followed the retreating Dickinson. The winning jockey approached, and the group crowded in to congratulate him. In the commotion, Erwin noticed Dickinson had drifted away.

"Charles!" he called. He motioned for his son-in-law to return, but Dickinson kept walking. "Excuse me, gentlemen," Erwin said quickly. "Rachel, it's a pleasure to see you."

Erwin hurried after Dickinson as the group began to disperse. Overton watched them go, his eyes fixed on

Dickinson, the earlier remark still burning in his mind. Jackson rested a hand at the small of Rachel's back and gently guided her away from the rail. "Perhaps we should call on Truxton while we're here."

Rachel's face brightened. She smiled wide, and together they turned toward the stables. As they walked, Jackson glanced back and caught the unease still lingering on Overton's face.

"John," he said, "care to see the fastest horse in Tennessee?"

Overton managed a smile, careful to keep it in place. "Of course."

Jackson gestured toward the stables, pointing out a pair of horses as they passed. Overton followed along, his steps measured, his attention elsewhere. Rachel spoke quietly to him, remarking on one of the horses. Overton nodded in reply, murmured something agreeable. But the words barely registered. His thoughts were still on Dickinson's slanderous remark.

♦♦♦♦♦♦

A week later, the City Hotel was quieter, though never truly calm. Smoke hung in a stagnant layer in the air, and the low murmur of voices drifted between the scattered tables. Andrew Jackson sat with Thomas Overton and John Coffee, a drink in his hand, laughing heartily as Coffee recounted the details of the duel with McNairy. Coffee slapped a hand against his injured leg and laughed, while Jackson shook his head in amusement. Thomas Overton listened in a state of lingering disbelief as the story unfolded.

John Overton paused just inside the entrance, scanning the tables. When he spotted Jackson, his expression tightened. Jackson lifted a hand in greeting. "Come on over here, John! Have a seat."

John Coffee smiled, remaining seated as he shook the judge's hand.

"I can't stay very long," Overton said. He didn't sit right away; instead, he paused and looked Coffee over. "It's good to see you. You appear to be doing well, all things considered."

Coffee shifted his weight in the chair. "It still pains me," he said, then laughed the comment off. "But that's to be expected. You saw the papers?"

Overton let out a short chuckle. "I did. Though I haven't seen Mr. McNairy."

That drew a round of genuine laughter from the table. Jackson, especially, was tickled by the remark and let out a hearty laugh of his own. "I do not believe you will," Jackson said.

Then Overton's expression shifted as he turned back to him. "You've made your peace with Joe, have you not?"

Jackson nodded once, his amusement still lingering.

"And his son-in-law?" Overton pressed.

Jackson's brow creased. "Why?"

Overton drew a deep breath. "He was speaking ill of Rachel at the track."

The words landed with quiet, devastating force. Jackson's expression darkened instantly as the meaning settled in. His posture stiffened, and color rose in his face, a jagged anger coming on fast and hot.

"I told him that his conduct was improper," Overton continued, "but he turned his back on me and walked away."

Jackson leaned forward, his voice dropping into a dangerous register. "And what was his reply?"

"The same thing you've heard time and again since your marriage," Overton said grimly. "I wish someone would find a new way to insult you."

Jackson shook his head and brought his fist down hard on the table, rattling the glasses until they jumped. "That sanctimonious rascal has trouble coming his way," he said. "I've held my tongue out of respect for Joe, but if he cannot rein in his son-in-law, he'll have cause to regret it."

Coffee and the Overtons exchanged uneasy looks, unsure how to answer the heat in his voice. Jackson drew a sharp breath, then asked, "John—what was his name?"

"It's Charles," Overton said.

"He'd best keep that young man at home," Jackson said, "or God help him." He lifted his glass and drained it in one motion. "Thomas, fetch me another drink!"

Thomas hesitated only a second; Jackson's anger had a way of filling a room until there was little air left for anyone else. Then Thomas rose and went quickly to the bar.

♦♦♦♦♦♦

The next afternoon, Andrew Jackson arrived at Clover Bottom with Thomas Overton at his side. He quickly spotted Joseph Erwin and Charles Dickinson near the rail, their attention fixed on a race in progress. Jackson marched toward them, but Overton caught his arm, slowing him down.

"Joe is your friend," Overton said quietly, his voice a steadying anchor. "Please be civil."

Jackson looked at him for a moment longer, then drew a slow, deliberate breath. Overton released his grip, and Jackson strode forward.

"Young man," Jackson said, stopping directly in front of Dickinson. His voice was controlled, but it held a jagged hardness. "Might I have a word?"

As Overton and Erwin exchanged awkward, forced pleasantries to mask the intrusion, Jackson guided Dickinson away from the rail and toward the stables. The noise of the crowd dulled as they moved, the space closing in around them until the smell of hay and horses replaced the excitement of the track. Erwin watched them go, unable to tear his eyes from his son-in-law.

Once they were alone, Jackson stopped and turned fully to face him. "Have you something to say to me?"

Dickinson blinked, his expression carefully blank as he played at being confused. Jackson's jaw tightened. "It's been said you've made remarks about my wife. Do you deny it?"

His voice carried farther than he had intended. Across the grass, both Erwin and Overton stared, drawn by the sudden, sharp spike of tension.

"I do not recall speaking ill of Mrs. Jackson," Dickinson said, his voice light.

"I know it to be true," Jackson replied, his gaze

unblinking.

Dickinson shifted under that stare. "General, Joe and I shared a drink upon arriving at the track. If I said anything at all," he added carefully, "it was meant in jest."

A heavy silence settled between them. Jackson continued to stare, the pause stretching long enough to make the excuse sound foolish even to the man who had spoken it.

"Jest?" Jackson finally said. "As a gentleman, you will not impugn my wife's honor. Are we agreed?"

Dickinson swallowed hard. "The bourbon flowed freely. I may have spoken out of turn. I offer my apologies for the offense."

Jackson glared at him, the heat of his anger still simmering. Behind them, Erwin craned his neck, desperate to read the body language of the confrontation.

"Is Mrs. Jackson present?" Dickinson asked, attempting to recover his footing. "I would offer her my apologies directly."

Something in Jackson shifted at the request. The fire cooled, just enough to allow the moment to pass. "I bear no quarrel with you or your family. Still, you would do well to watch your words where my wife is concerned."

Dickinson paused for a half second, clearly fighting his own rising temper. "Yes, sir," he said.

Jackson extended his hand, and Dickinson took it. The handshake was brief, formal, and entirely empty.

They returned to Overton and Erwin together. Dickinson said nothing, his jaw tight and irritation simmering just beneath the surface of his skin.

"Shall we watch the races?" Jackson said casually,

as if nothing had happened at all.

The four men moved back toward the rail in a line of uneasy camaraderie. Under his breath, Erwin leaned toward Dickinson. "What was that exchange about?"

Dickinson's mouth tightened as he kept walking, his eyes fixed straight ahead. "He thinks I'm beneath his notice," he muttered. A dark light flickered in his eyes. "He is mistaken."

Erwin glanced over at him, confused, a sudden flicker of genuine concern crossing his face.

"I Shall Have His Life"

A few days later, the courthouse hallway buzzed with voices and foot traffic. Lawyers clustered in small groups, trading stories and sharp opinions before court was called to order. Charles Dickinson stood at the center of one such circle, holding court with an easy, practiced confidence. His posture was relaxed, his voice carrying just far enough to draw the attention of those passing by. Nearby, Thomas Swann, still visibly battered, hovered close, nodding eagerly and laughing too loudly in support.

"Mrs. Jackson said her husband's horse would leave Ploughboy well behind," Dickinson was saying. "That's when I told her — about as far out of sight as she left her first husband when she went off with the General."

Laughter rippled through the group. Everyone laughed, except for John Overton.

Overton had just stepped into the hallway. He took in the scene at a glance and walked straight toward Dickinson. "Good morning, Charles," he said evenly. "Might I see you in my chambers?"

The laughter died instantly. Swann and the other lawyers drifted off at once, suddenly finding other places they needed to be. Dickinson followed Overton down the hall, his confidence intact and his face set in an unreadable mask.

Inside Judge Overton's chambers, the door closed softly behind them. Overton moved to his desk and sat, his fingers resting on the polished wood as he searched for the right place to begin. Dickinson took the chair opposite him, settling in as though this were an interview he fully expected to pass.

"Charles…" Overton began, then paused again, noticing that the young lawyer's smug expression hadn't changed. He tried another angle. "I've had occasion to speak with my colleagues. Your training speaks well of you. Justice Marshall is a wise man."

"Yes," Dickinson said, clearly pleased. "He's a man of remarkable intellect. I count myself fortunate to have studied under him."

"In a few years," Overton continued, "you may one day sit here yourself. Your prospects as a jurist are strong."

Dickinson smirked. He knew it; he'd always known it.

"But," Overton said, his voice growing firmer, "this matter between you and the General does you no good. He has friends you would not wish to make enemies of."

"Oh?" Dickinson said lightly. "Such as the governor?"

Overton chuckled despite himself. "It's true Governor Sevier and the General are not on friendly terms. But Mr. Jefferson, our President, holds Andrew Jackson in high esteem." He leaned forward slightly. "This matter between your father-in-law and Andrew has gone too far."

Overton paused, but Dickinson's expression didn't change. He remained smug, certain of himself.

"Could the General have acted with more restraint?" Overton continued. "He is a proud man, and he took some satisfaction in watching Joe struggle over the payment. But your father-in-law hung himself; he simply made the error of placing the rope in the General's hands."

Dickinson scoffed. "He thinks far too highly of himself."

"Andrew Jackson is quite a complicated man," Overton said. "I hold him in high regard, but he has his faults. I would never have made such a wager on a horse race."

Dickinson rolled his eyes, the gesture quick and dismissive.

"I've known Joe a long time," Overton continued. "Had the roles been reversed, he'd have done the same — and Andrew would have been the one left to bear it."

"I don't know what he would have done," Dickinson said flatly.

Overton's expression hardened, the professional warmth leaving his voice. "Rachel Jackson is a close friend of mine. I've known her longer than I've known Andrew. Her first husband, Lewis, was not an honorable man. He was cruel."

Overton's gaze held Dickinson now, unblinking. "When I lived in Harrodsburg, I boarded with his family," he said quietly. "I saw his brutality firsthand." Overton's voice lowered even further. "Lewis was given to drink. And when he drank, he grew violent."

Dickinson did not interrupt, but he barely reacted.

"One night I saw him strike her," Overton continued. "I stepped in to stop it. He threw me across a table, and then turned back to her." Overton paused and sighed, the sound tired and sad. "He beat her so severely that she was never able to bear children. After she returned to Nashville, he petitioned the court in Mercer County for a divorce. We believed it had been granted. I even assisted Rachel with the papers myself."

Another pause. A frustrated breath.

"Somehow the papers were never signed by a judge. The divorce was never finalized. I did not know. Nor did she." Overton looked at Dickinson then, searching his face for some sign of feeling. "She met Andrew not long after. They came to love one another. And I am glad, truly glad, that she found him. Andrew treats her well. Neither of them deserves to be spoken of with contempt."

He leaned forward, pressing the point. "They are not living in bigamy. They are the victims of a clerk's neglect or of a drunkard who never signed what was required. Either way, it is of no consequence. It amounts to nothing more than a defect in the law between a man and a woman who love one another." Overton gestured toward Dickinson. "You are newly married. You know what such affection means."

Dickinson's smirk finally faltered. Annoyance flashed across his face and his jaw tightened before he looked away.

"Charles," Overton said softly, "do not rouse his temper. Andrew is a gentleman, but his anger is not to be tested. You saw what became of Mr. Swann. Let this go, I ask it of you."

Dickinson sighed. "I'm obliged to you, Judge Overton. I will consider your counsel. Court awaits me."

"Yes," Overton replied. "Very well."

Dickinson left the chambers. Overton turned back to the papers on his desk, but before he could refocus, a voice carried clearly down the hallway.

"Mr. Benton!"

Overton froze.

"Charles," Thomas Benton's voice replied, "is it true that you struck General Jackson at the race track, in the presence of his wife?"

Overton listened, a cold dread settling in his chest.

"No, no," Dickinson said easily. "It did not come to that. He saw my temper rising and withdrew like a coward."

Benton let out a low laugh. "Oh my," he said, clearly impressed.

Overton closed his eyes. His head dropped into his hands as he sighed deeply. Thomas Benton passed the open doorway and noticed the judge inside. He slowed, then leaned in, poking his head through the doorframe.

"Good afternoon, Judge."

Overton didn't look up. Benton paused, his eyebrows lifting slightly at the sight, then moved on down the hallway. He left Overton exactly where he was — alone with the trouble he knew was only beginning.

◆◆◆◆◆◆

The City Hotel was loud again that night, thick with the scent of strong drink and the hum of overlapping conversations. Andrew Jackson sat at his usual table with Thomas Overton and John Coffee, a glass held loosely in his hand.

"When are you going to run Truxton?" Coffee asked, leaning back.

"I don't know," Jackson said. "Joe tells me Ploughboy will be fit in a few weeks. I'd like to see the matter settled at last." A thin, predatory smile crossed his face. "I wouldn't object to winning more of Joe's money."

Coffee laughed, and Jackson joined him, but Thomas Overton remained silent.

"Do you think the matter was made clear to Joe's son-in-law?" Coffee asked.

"If that pup ever speaks her sacred name again," Jackson said, his voice instantly hardening, "he will regret it."

Coffee nodded. "There's something about him. He thinks the world belongs to him. He will learn soon enough to mind his words among grown men."

Thomas Overton continued to stare into his drink, his silence becoming a weight at the table. Jackson noticed. "Thomas, you've barely touched your glass."

Thomas shifted uneasily. "Andrew…"

Jackson leaned forward, watching his friend closely.

"I was speaking with some attorneys," Thomas said, finally looking up. "It seems Dickinson hasn't learned his lesson. He's still speaking openly—about your marriage. Worse than that, he told people at the courthouse he'd lick you if you ever crossed him again."

Jackson leaned back and drew a long, slow breath through his nose. The fire was there, visible and dangerous in his eyes, but for the moment, he held it down.

"He's a coward," Jackson said.

Coffee's eyes widened slightly. He knew that tone; he knew the specific frequency of Jackson's voice that usually preceded a storm.

"I'm going to settle this," Jackson stated.

"You must remain calm," Thomas said quickly,

reaching out as if to anchor him.

But Jackson was already on his feet. He pushed his chair back with a sharp scrape and strode toward the door. Coffee and Thomas Overton exchanged a long look, saying nothing, the air between them thick with the realization of what was coming.

As Jackson reached the entrance, John Overton stepped inside, nearly colliding with him. "Andrew! Where are you going?"

"I have business to attend to," Jackson said, already attempting to brush past him.

Overton raised his hands in a silent plea for a halt. "We need to talk."

"I'm done talking," Jackson snapped, his restraint snapping. "That boy has taken on more than he can bear."

"I spoke with him briefly," Overton said, his voice low and urgent. "He's only a young man, Andrew. I will see him tomorrow and speak some sense into him."

Jackson paused for only a fraction of a second. "You'd better."

"Why don't you sit down," Overton said carefully, "and have a drink?"

Still fuming, Jackson shook his head and pushed out into the night, the cool air doing nothing to dampen the heat of his rage. John Overton stood there for a moment, watching the door swing shut, then crossed the room to where his brother and Coffee sat. Both men were staring into space, already knowing the evening had slipped beyond anyone's control.

◆◆◆◆◆◆

The next morning, the courthouse was already stirring with its usual restless energy. Thomas Overton walked the corridor with a grim purpose until he spotted Charles Dickinson. The younger man was seated on a bench beside Thomas Swann, the two of them bent low over a sheaf of papers.

"Good morning," Thomas said, stopping before them.

Dickinson looked up, his expression guarded. "Mr. Overton."

Thomas didn't waste time easing into the conversation. "It's not wise to speak against the Major General of the Tennessee Militia. Word has reached him."

"Good," Dickinson said coolly. He rose to his feet, gathering his papers with slow, deliberate movements. "Am I meant to be intimidated? That man is a scoundrel. If he wants satisfaction, I will give it to him. Why does he send you and your brother to lecture me? He knows where to find me. Let him come himself."

Beside him, Swann sneered, clearly savoring the defiance. His disdain for Jackson was plain as he nodded along, cheering Dickinson on without saying a word. Thomas glanced at Swann, then back to Dickinson, the sheer brazenness of the young man catching him off guard.

Dickinson turned away abruptly and strode down the hallway, with Swann scrambling to keep pace behind him. Heads turned as they passed; a few conversations stalled in their wake.

"Charles!" Thomas Overton called after him, but it was useless. At the far end of the hall, a heavy door swung open and Dickinson disappeared through it.

John Overton appeared then, drawn by his

brother's raised voice. He came to Thomas's side, following his gaze down the empty corridor. "What ails that young man?" Thomas asked, still visibly shaken.

John frowned. "Where is he going? I told Andrew I would speak with him."

But Dickinson was already gone, and whatever restraint remained in the building seemed to leave with him. He burst out of the courthouse and into the street with Swann close at his shoulder. Their pace was quick and purposeful as Swann fed the fire with every step.

"The General thinks himself above reproach," Swann said bitterly. He turned his head, gesturing to his battered face where the bruises were still dark and swollen. "Look at me. No redress. Not so much as a word spoken against him. And now he sends others to chastise you, as though you were a schoolboy."

Dickinson walked with his jaw tight, looking as though he were chewing on nails. His anger had nowhere to go yet, and it was eating at him from the inside.

Swann kept at it. "He thinks he may shame you without consequence."

Dickinson's teeth ground together. "I shall have his life."

Swann's mouth curled in satisfaction as they rounded the corner and stopped in front of a modest brick building—the offices of *The Impartial Review*. Inside, the newspaper office smelled of ink, fresh paper, and hot metal. Dickinson and Swann entered with an unmistakable air of authority. A lone reporter sat hunched over a desk, absorbed in a story, and looked up as they approached.

"Good morning, Mr. Dickinson!" the reporter said, offering a polite smile.

Dickinson walked straight to the desk and stood over him. "Where's Stanley?"

"He's working on the afternoon edition," the reporter said cautiously. "How may I be of service?"

"Go fetch him."

The reporter stalled, his eyes glancing back at his unfinished work.

"Now."

The reporter scrambled to his feet and disappeared into the back office. Moments later, Stanley Black hurried out. He was short, graying, and already looking nervous. "Charles, what can I do for you, sir?"

Dickinson handed him a piece of paper. Stanley's eyes moved across the page, back and forth, faster and faster as his face drained of all color. "I cannot print this," Stanley said quietly.

"My family owns this newspaper," Dickinson replied coldly. "You will print what I place before you."

"Sir," Stanley began, swallowing hard, "calling General Jackson a…" He stopped and read the lines again. "A worthless scoundrel, a poltroon, and a coward… this will result in grave consequences."

Dickinson glanced at Swann, then fixed Stanley with a glare that shut the man down completely.

"Is Mr. Erwin in agreement with this?" Stanley asked, his voice barely above a whisper.

That did it.

"This will be printed tomorrow," Dickinson snapped. "See that it is done."

Stanley nodded stiffly. "Yes, sir. I will prepare the press." He looked down at the note one more time, disbelief etched across his face, then hurried away, already knowing the city would be talking by morning.

Dickinson and Swann grinned at one another, satisfied with their morning's work. "I long to see his response," Swann said.

Dickinson chuckled, a low and pleased sound.

In the next room, Stanley Black went to work. He laid out the article by hand, letter by letter, the slow, deliberate labor of typesetting. He paused more than once, shaking his head as his eyes moved over the venomous words. He couldn't believe what he was assembling, but his hands kept moving. Lead type clicked into place. The press was prepared.

When it was finished, Stanley pulled the first sheet free and held it up. He read it again, as if hoping the ink might rearrange itself into something less lethal. Then he folded the paper under his arm and left the office without another word.

Judge Overton sat in his chambers, his head bowed as he reviewed a stack of documents, when an urgent, heavy knock struck the door.

"Come in."

The door cracked open and Stanley Black slipped inside. He looked sheepish and profoundly uneasy. "Judge, please forgive the intrusion," Stanley said, his voice low. "But there is a matter of some urgency I must bring to you."

"Please," Overton said, already sensing the shape of the trouble. "Come in, Stanley."

Stanley shuffled across the room and took the chair

opposite the desk. Without a word, he reached into his coat and handed Overton a fresh sheet of paper.

Overton's eyes moved across the page. As he read, the color drained from his face, leaving him looking suddenly older.

"Mr. Erwin's son-in-law gave me this letter," Stanley said quietly. "It will be in the paper tomorrow morning."

Overton continued to stare at the sheet, then looked up at Stanley. He knew at once what this meant; he didn't need a law book to tell him the outcome. "You mustn't print this, Stanley," Overton said.

"I have no choice."

"You cannot!"

"His father-in-law owns the newspaper."

"But Stanley..."

Stanley ran a hand through his hair, exhaling a sharp, frustrated breath. "Sir, I cannot refuse Mr. Dickinson's request."

Overton leaned back, rubbing his forehead as the consequences raced through his mind. "Please," he said, his voice trembling slightly. "Someone will be hurt—or killed. That young man does not understand what he's set in motion. It will not be Andrew alone who reads this; all of Nashville will see it. He'll be left no choice but to answer it. This will lead to bloodshed."

He looked up, the desperation plain in his eyes. "Stanley, please..."

"I am sorry," Stanley said, his own voice thick with regret. "I wanted you to give the General word before it appears tomorrow. I did not wish him to be taken unawares."

"Oh, Stanley," Overton murmured, the paper

crinkling in his grip. "Then there's no stopping it now."

Stanley rose and left the room as quietly as he had entered. Overton remained seated, staring straight ahead at the far wall. He held the paper in his hands with a grim certainty, knowing that a line had finally been crossed and that there was no longer any way to step back from it.

The Bar of Honor

A few hours later, the large log cabin by the Cumberland River was warm with lamplight and the sound of easy laughter. Andrew Jackson was down on all fours, serving as a pony for his four-year-old nephew, Andy Donelson, who rode him triumphantly around the room. Rachel stood nearby, her face lit with a smile as the boy shouted.

"Faster, Uncle!"

Jackson obliged, picking up the pace as Andy howled with delight.

"Slower, Andrew!" Rachel called, half-laughing and half-scolding.

The door opened and John Overton stepped inside. Jackson looked up, surprised to see his friend at so late an hour. Rachel caught the look on Overton's face and tilted her head, immediately sensing the shift in the air. She hurried over and scooped Andy into her arms to quiet him.

"Andrew," Overton said, his voice heavy. "Good evening, Rachel. Please accept my apologies. I know it is late."

Jackson rose to his feet, brushing the dust from his knees, and shook his friend's hand. "John, what are you doing out here at this hour?"

"It's urgent," Overton said. "It could not wait until morning."

Rachel didn't ask questions; she knew the look of men's business. She ushered the boy toward the door, giving the men their privacy. As Andy was carried off, he twisted around in her arms and stuck out his tongue at

Jackson. Jackson grinned and stuck his tongue out right back.

"Andy! Andrew!" Rachel laughed. "Stop it. Come now. I will leave you two alone."

They disappeared through the door, the sound of the child's fading laughter leaving a sudden, ringing silence in the room. Jackson's expression hardened the moment they were gone. "What is so pressing?"

Overton handed him a folded paper. "This will be in *The Impartial Review* tomorrow. I thought it best you see it before it goes to print."

Jackson read in a chilling silence. His face betrayed nothing—no flicker of anger, no wideness of the eye. When he finished, he looked at Overton, then quietly crossed the room to the window and stared out into the pitch-black night.

"What is to be done?" Overton asked.

Without turning around, Jackson spoke to the glass. "Will you see that young rascal tomorrow at the courthouse?"

"I cannot be certain he'll be there," Overton replied carefully. "But I do see him often."

Jackson moved to a small desk and sat. He dipped his quill, and the soft, rhythmic scratching of it was the only sound left in the cabin.

> *Your conduct and expressions relative to me of late have been of such a nature and so insulting that require and shall have my notice. I hope, sir, your courage will be an ample security to me that I will obtain speedily that satisfaction due me for the insults offered, and in the way my friend who hands you this will point out. He waits upon you for that purpose, and with your friend will enter into immediate arrangements*

for this purpose.

When the note was finished, Jackson handed it to Overton. The judge read it in the flickering lamplight, then looked up, his voice heavy with a final plea. "You need not go down this road, Andrew. You were once young and foolish yourself. Think better of it."

Jackson slowly shook his head, his face a mask of cold certainty. "I was never this foolish."

"That young man is beneath you," Overton said quietly. "He is of no consequence."

"For malicious slander," Jackson replied, "all men are answered only at the bar of honor."

Overton said nothing. His eyes searched Jackson's, pleading with his friend to reconsider, but he found only the iron-willed General.

"Will you deliver it for me?" Jackson asked.

Overton hesitated. "I will let you know his reply."

Jackson knew his friend wanted no part of this, but he also knew Overton's loyalty was absolute. "John," he said softly. "Thank you."

He patted Overton on the back. The judge nodded once and let himself out into the night. Jackson stood alone for a moment in the sudden quiet, then turned and walked into the other room. The echoes of the laughter from earlier still seemed to linger in the air, but they were now replaced by something colder and far more dangerous.

In the adjoining room, Rachel sat on the settee with Andy curled beside her, reading aloud from a book. Jackson entered quietly and crossed to her, bending to kiss her forehead with a tenderness that betrayed nothing of the letter he had just signed. He smiled at the boy and reached down to ruffle his hair.

"What did John wish to speak with you about?" Rachel asked, looking up from the page.

"A small matter at the track," Jackson said, his voice smooth and untroubled. "It requires my attention."

He moved to the window and stared out into the dark, his thoughts already miles away on a field in Kentucky. Andy slid off the chair and ran over, tugging at his uncle's leg. Jackson scooped the boy up and spun him playfully, drawing a bright burst of laughter from the child.

Rachel smiled at the sight, but she knew her husband well enough to recognize the shadow behind his eyes. She knew something was wrong.

◆◆◆◆◆◆

The next morning, the Nashville courthouse buzzed with a sharp, restless energy. Charles Dickinson sat comfortably in a wooden chair with Thomas Swann at his side, surrounded by a dozen men who leaned in close, copies of the morning paper in their hands.

"How do you think the General will respond when he sees your letter?" one attorney asked, grinning.

Dickinson snickered, leaning back with practiced ease. "No doubt he'll dispatch another friend to express his distress." He paused, squinting at the ceiling as if giving the matter serious thought. "In fact," he added, "I believe it's Mr. Coffee's turn to call on me."

Dickinson snickered again, and Swann doubled over, his forced laughter barking through the corridor.

Down the hall, John Overton appeared. His face was a mask of grim resolve, the skin tight over his cheekbones. The laughter and murmurs continued unabated as he approached the group.

"Mr. Dickinson," Overton said, his voice cutting cleanly through the noise. "May I speak with you in my chambers?"

Dickinson rose at once, smoothed his coat, and offered a dismissive wave to his companions. "Pardon me, gentlemen."

Every eye in the hallway followed the two men as they walked in silence toward the judge's office. Inside, Overton closed the door, the click of the latch sounding final in the quiet room. He took his seat behind the heavy desk.

"Please, sit down."

Dickinson sat across from him, looking more like a man waiting for a toast than a reprimand.

"I would have you know," Overton said, his voice carefully measured, "I did all that lay within my power to prevent this." He reached into his jacket and produced a folded letter, sliding it across the wood.

Dickinson read the challenge and then laughed. "Judge," he said brightly, "may I borrow your quill? I shall answer his letter at once."

Overton blinked, the sheer recklessness of the young man momentarily stunning him. "Would you not think on it for a few days?"

Dickinson shook his head.

"Perhaps consult with your father-in-law…"

"No need."

Overton stared at him for a long beat, then slowly opened a drawer and slid a quill across the desk. Dickinson didn't hesitate. He dipped the nib and began writing at once, the scratching of the pen the only sound left in the room.

Sir,
Your note of this morning is received, and your request shall be gratified. My friend who hands you this will make the necessary arrangements.
I am,
Charles Dickinson.

He handed the letter back. Overton glanced at it, the ink still wet, then folded it with trembling fingers and slipped it into his coat.

"If he wants satisfaction," Dickinson said, standing now and smoothing the front of his waistcoat, "he can find it on the Red River. The place where Mr. Coffee and Mr. McNairy met. We both know it cannot take place here. I have important cases next week. Perhaps the twenty-ninth or thirtieth will be satisfactory."

Overton looked up at him, the alarm written clearly across his weathered face. "Is this truly what you wish? A duel with the General? Someone may be killed, Charles."

Dickinson didn't flinch. Instead, he grinned — a sharp, confident expression that made Overton's stomach turn.

"You could be killed," Overton pressed, his voice rising with a final, desperate plea for sanity.

"Please deliver my message," Dickinson said coolly, already moving toward the door. "Let me know when the General wishes to meet me."

He turned and walked out of the chambers without another word.

Overton remained seated in the sudden, oppressive silence of his office. Then, he pulled the letter back out and reread it. The reality of what he had just helped set in motion settled heavily upon him, the paper feeling like lead in his hands.

♦♦♦♦♦♦

The City Hotel was lively that night, but the table where Andrew Jackson sat with John Coffee and the Overton brothers was notably subdued. The air around them seemed to thicken as Jackson broke the long silence.

"I have agreed to the duel," he said evenly. "Joe's son-in-law."

No one needed clarification. The name had been haunting their conversations for weeks. Jackson turned his gaze toward Thomas Overton. "I ask that you serve as my second." Then, his eyes flicking momentarily toward Coffee's bandaged, injured leg, he added, "I would ask John, but…"

Coffee stood, his jaw set as he leaned heavily on his cane. "I can still get about," he said stubbornly, before turning to make his slow, halting way toward the bar.

Thomas shifted in his chair, the gravity of the request settling on his shoulders. "What are the duties of a second?"

John Overton answered before Jackson could find the words. "You will settle the terms. You will act as intermediary between Charles and his second on the day of the meeting."

Jackson continued, his voice calm, almost instructional, as if he were discussing a land survey rather than a killing. "You will determine the distance between us and give the word to fire. If I fall, it will be your responsibility to tend to me and see that I reach a doctor."

Thomas's eyes widened. The reality of the role hit him then; this was not mere ceremony. This was a grim, essential duty.

"Charles's second should arrive soon," John Overton noted, his eyes scanning the door. "Andrew, please be polite."

Jackson smirked faintly and dipped his head in a mock-deferential gesture. "Yes, Your Honor."

John shot him a sharp, warning look.

"What should I bring?" Thomas asked, his voice tighter now.

"We will be staying overnight in Kentucky," Jackson replied. "You will need clothes. I shall bring the pistol."

John Overton hesitated, the judge in him warring with the friend. He asked quietly, "That young attorney is expecting a child, Andrew. Are you truly prepared to take the life of a man soon to be a father? What is to be gained by it?"

Jackson didn't hesitate. The answer was already forged. "Gain?" he said. "I have but one thing to lose, sir — my honor."

The words hung between them, stark and absolute,

while the rest of the bar roared on, oblivious to the lethal machinery that had already been set in motion.

A man approached the table, Dr. Hanson Catlet. He was slender, well-dressed, and carried himself with a practiced, clinical composure. "I beg your pardon, General Jackson I presume?"

Jackson studied the stranger for a silent moment before nodding.

"Sir, I am Hanson Catlet. I will serve as Charles's second. I regret that our acquaintance is made under such circumstances."

Jackson rose and shook his hand, his manner cordial and measured. "Please, take a seat."

"Mr. Catlet," John Overton said, "Charles told me that he wishes to meet at the Red River near Mr. Harrison's mill. Have we determined the date?"

"If it is agreeable, we ask to meet on Friday, May 30th, at dawn."

John Overton glanced at Jackson, who gave a slow, somber nod. "Yes, that will do," Jackson said calmly. "There is an inn not far from there where Thomas and I may lodge." Jackson gestured toward Thomas. "Mr. Overton will be my second."

Catlet hesitated, momentarily confused as his eyes moved from the Judge to Thomas.

"Given John's position on the Superior Court, he cannot be seen in any part of this," Jackson explained. "If you require anything, you may speak with Thomas."

"Thank you," Catlet said, leaning in. "One last point—if you'll indulge me. You do intend to use pistols, correct? I do not believe Charles owns a broadsword."

Catlet chuckled nervously, and for a second, the tension broke. Jackson was genuinely amused. "I do have the longer arms. Broadswords might suit me well enough."

Thomas blinked, looking between them. "Are you comfortable wielding a sword?"

Jackson laughed. "No, I prefer pistols."

"Pistols it is," Catlet said. A subdued ripple of laughter moved around the table, a brief respite from the gravity of their business. Catlet stood, then paused. "I hope this may yet be resolved without bloodshed. I've urged Charles to delope, though he's not agreed to it. I sincerely hope you both return safely to your homes."

Jackson offered a polite, distant smile. "Thank you, Mr. Catlet."

Catlet nodded and turned to Thomas. "Mr. Overton, I will speak to you soon."

As Catlet departed, John Overton leaned back, his eyes narrowing. "Have you considered this fully; what follows if you prevail? Charles and his wife are expecting a child. Word of it will surely reach Washington."

Jackson shifted in his chair, but his gaze remained fixed.

"And what do you suppose your friend Mr. Jefferson will make of it?" Overton pressed. "That the commander of the Tennessee militia should leave his post and cross into another state, not in defense of country or law, but to hunt down a man over a slight to his pride? Is this the conduct of a public officer, or of a hot-blooded duelist who mistakes personal affront for justice?"

Jackson stared into the amber liquid of his glass, saying nothing. Finally, he spoke. "It is about respect — mine and hers."

"Respect won't save you from being cast out of the militia," Overton snapped. "Or worse, losing the

President's trust. Consider your future, Andrew!"

Jackson ground his teeth, his eyes fixed. John Overton exhaled sharply, a sound of profound frustration. "There is yet time to step back from this…"

Jackson sighed and drained his glass in one motion.

Across the room, as Catlet made his way toward the exit, John Coffee stood at the bar. He recognized the newcomer at once. "Dr. Catlet!"

Catlet stopped short and turned, searching Coffee's face. "Coffee, John Coffee," the big man said, stepping closer. "I recall our card game at the Knoxville tavern a few weeks ago. You left the table with more of my coin than I care to remember."

Recognition clicked, and Catlet broke into a warm laugh. "Yes, Mr. Coffee. Nice to see you."

"What brings you to Nashville?"

Catlet's smile faltered slightly. "I have been asked to be the second in a duel."

Coffee's expression changed instantly. "When we last spoke, you told me you had served as a second before. Your friend, the marksman…"

"Indeed," Catlet said. "He is not much given to restraint."

Coffee's brow furrowed as the pieces began to assemble themselves in his mind. "Have you come to see the General? And are you acquainted with Mr. Dickinson?"

Catlet nodded.

Coffee hesitated, a cold dread pooling in his stomach. "How many times has he stood in the field?"

Catlet hesitated, then began counting slowly on his fingers until he reached eight.

Coffee swallowed a hard lump in his throat. "Has any man walked away from him?"

Slowly, one by one, Catlet curled his fingers back into his palm until his hands were tight, silent fists. "The matter was settled before his shot could be answered."

Behind them, Jackson crossed the room toward the door, his coat already in hand. Coffee turned just in time to see his friend leave, the silhouette of the General disappearing into the night. For a brief, helpless moment, he wondered if it would be one of the last times he saw him alive.

"I had hoped Mr. Dickinson and General Jackson might yet find some other means of accommodation," Catlet said. "But the General appears resolved upon the duel." He pulled out his pocket watch and checked the time. "Mr. Coffee, it has been a pleasure to see you again. If you will excuse me, I must speak with Mr. Dickinson."

Catlet patted Coffee on the back and exited. Coffee didn't hesitate. He hobbled back toward the table, the dread climbing his spine until it choked him.

"Thomas!"

♦ ♦ ♦ ♦ ♦ ♦

Catlet left the City Hotel and walked several blocks through the cool Nashville night. He ducked into Winn's Tavern, where the air was a stagnant fog of tobacco smoke and raw, drunken bravado.

Inside, the place was alive, vibrating with a different energy than the Hotel. Catlet scanned the room and quickly spotted Charles Dickinson at the bar. He was surrounded by Thomas Swann and a small knot of young attorneys who were hanging on his every word as if he were delivering a closing argument.

"Men speak of Jackson as if he were immune to consequence," Dickinson said, his voice carrying with practiced authority. "I am not persuaded that such immunity exists."

Swann leaned in eagerly, his eyes bright with reflected ambition. "Felling him would make your name, Charles!"

The other attorneys leaned in, impressed, grinning as if they were already witnessing a turning point in history.

"Precisely," Dickinson said, warming to the attention of his peers.

Cheers and approving murmurs rippled through the group as Catlet approached the circle. Dickinson turned and spotted him at once, his face lighting up. "Have you made the arrangements?"

Catlet nodded, though his expression remained grave. "Friday, just as you requested. No swords. Pistols at the Red River."

Dickinson beamed, his confidence radiating outward. Beside him, Swann's grin sharpened into something jagged.

Catlet hesitated, looking at the young, eager faces around the bar. "There is still time to make peace, Charles."

Dickinson scoffed, playing to his audience with a look of mock offense. "No. There will be no peace with that scoundrel." He tapped the wood of the bar in front of Catlet. "Thomas — Dr. Catlet needs a drink."

Catlet slid onto a stool, feeling a profound sense of

unease. As Swann flagged down the barkeep, the crowd pressed in closer, already drinking in a future that had not yet been earned.

Goodbye

The following morning, the large log cabin by the river was quiet, the early light filtering in pale, dusty shafts through the windows.

Andrew Jackson walked down the hall and stopped short when he saw Rachel standing at the window. Her arms were wrapped tightly around herself. He came up behind her and wrapped his arms around her shoulders, seeking to offer comfort, but she didn't relax. She felt cold beneath his touch.

"I saw what that young man wrote in the newspaper."

Jackson opened his mouth to speak, but no words came. The silence stretched, heavy and suffocating.

"You need not go."

She turned to him then, tears already spilling over her cheeks. "An insult fades," she said, her voice breaking. "A bullet does not. I cannot lose you to this." She reached for him, her hands trembling. "Please. Stay with me."

Jackson took her hand, his own eyes wet as he tried and failed to steady her.

"What will you do?" Rachel asked, pulling her hand free. "Answer every cruel tongue with violence?"

Something snapped in him then. The weariness of years of defense surged to the surface. "Every tavern I enter, I see their looks," Jackson said sharply. "I hear them whispering—questioning my name and yours." He drew a breath, his frame trembling with the effort of his restraint. "I will endure it no longer."

Rachel shook her head, her expression one of

profound grief. "Then you will spend your life at war."

"Conflict has followed me since I was a boy," Jackson said, his voice flat and final. "It will not end here."

Rachel turned away from him and stormed down the hall, leaving Jackson standing alone in the quiet cabin.

He remained there for a short time. Finally, he turned and walked to his desk. He opened the drawer, reached inside, and lifted out a heavy dueling pistol. Jackson laid it carefully on the desktop and stared at the cold steel, the weight of what lay ahead finally, unmistakably, before him.

◆ ◆ ◆ ◆ ◆ ◆

On the other side of Nashville, Peach Blossom Mansion sat bathed in the deceptive peace of the morning light.

Jane Dickinson sat by the window with a book lying open in her lap. One hand rested absently on the small, still-new swell of her belly, while the other turned a page. The door creaked softly.

Charles Dickinson entered, carrying a neatly packed traveling case. As he reached Jane, his sharp features softened. She glanced up and offered him a gentle, searching smile.

"I must be on my way now, my dear."

He bent and kissed her forehead. Jane closed her eyes for a moment, absorbing the touch, then looked up at him again. Her smile was thinning. "How long will you be gone?"

"Only a hearing in Kentucky," Dickinson said easily, his voice smooth and untroubled. "I shall return by tomorrow evening."

Jane studied his face, her intuition flickering. Something felt off, nothing she could name, just a quiet, cold unease that sat in the pit of her stomach.

"It's a simple matter," he added quickly, sensing her hesitation. "I will not be long."

He crouched beside her chair. "Is there anything you require before I go?"

She shook her head, her eyes still locked on his. "No. Only take care." Her voice was soft, edged with a worry she didn't quite understand. Charles covered her hand with his own and gave it a reassuring squeeze.

"Always."

He flashed her his familiar, brilliant smile. But as he straightened and turned toward the door, Jane's expression faltered. She watched him walk across the room, valise in hand.

"Charles?"

He stopped, his hand already resting on the brass doorknob.

"You will be home by tomorrow evening?"

There was the briefest hesitation. "Tomorrow evening," he said. "You have my word."

With one last smile, he opened the door and stepped out. It clicked shut behind him, leaving the room suddenly, oppressively still. Jane looked back down at her book, but the words blurred into meaningless black lines. Her gaze drifted instead to the window, where she could see Hanson Catlet and Uncle Bob waiting beside a wagon in the drive.

Outside, Charles descended the steps with a brisk purpose. Bob climbed up to the coach box as Catlet opened the wagon door and started inside.

"Charles!"

Joseph Erwin hurried forward, his face a map of anxiety. Dickinson stopped. Erwin approached the wagon, lowering his voice so the servants wouldn't overhear.

"My difficulties with the General are no concern of yours," Erwin said, his voice trembling. "Your letter has raised a storm of indignation. Whatever end you seek, I urge you—let the matter lie."

"Joe," Charles replied firmly, "no man will be permitted to slight my family. I care not whether the offender is Thomas Jefferson or Andrew Jackson. The General's words demand an answer."

"I know you are skilled with a pistol," Erwin said, his voice tightening with a father's desperation, "but this is no sport. A duel admits no second chance." He lowered his voice even further, his eyes darting toward the upstairs window. "Do not let passion govern you. I beg you! Consider your wife. Consider the child she carries."

For a fleeting, jagged moment, doubt crossed Charles's face. The armor of his hubris cracked. Then, as quickly as it had appeared, the doubt vanished. He squared his shoulders, his practiced confidence settling back into place like a mask.

"I shall return tomorrow night."

He placed a hand on Erwin's shoulder, a gesture that was meant to be a reassurance but felt more like a dismissal. "I will see it through," Dickinson said. "Andrew Jackson believes himself untouchable. No man is."

Charles climbed into the wagon, and Catlet followed. As the wheels began to churn the gravel and they rolled away, Erwin stood alone on the drive. He watched until the wagon disappeared from sight, a cold dread tightening in his chest.

◆◆◆◆◆◆

That night, the log cabin was quiet, the lamplight low and unsteady.

Andrew Jackson walked slowly down the hall until he stopped before a portrait of Rachel. He studied it for a long moment, as if committing her face to memory, then turned and entered his office.

The moment he stepped inside, his eyes went straight to the pistol resting on the desk. It seemed to pull at him. He crossed the room, lit a candle, and sat down. The flame steadied, throwing soft light across the walls.

Jackson's gaze lifted to a portrait of his mother watching from above. He opened a drawer and removed an old letter, creased from years of handling. As he read, her words echoed in his mind.

Andrew, in personal conduct, be always polite but never obsequious. None will respect you more than you respect yourself. Avoid quarrels as long as you can without yielding to imposition. But sustain your manhood always.

He steadied himself, his fingers clenching white-knuckled around the edge of the paper.

In the doorway behind him, Rachel appeared. She hesitated there, a shadow against the hall light, watching him in silence. The room felt heavy, crowded with things neither of them wanted to say. At last, she stepped inside, the floorboards groaning softly under her weight.

"You will be leaving in the morning?"

"I will."

She moved closer, her voice trembling with a fear that was barely contained. "You are not bound to this, Andrew."

Jackson sighed, still not looking up from the desk. "You know I cannot let it lie," he said. "It is not merely words." He paused, the silence stretching between them. "A man who will not answer an affront, who will not stand for what is his, ceases to be a man at all."

Rachel folded her arms tightly across her chest, a defensive posture against the cold reality of his words. Tears glistened in the candlelight, but she refused to let them fall.

Jackson's posture softened. His shoulders sagged slightly as he finally looked at her, his voice quiet but firm. "I made a promise to you… to myself. I won't let anyone tarnish your name."

She shook her head, her voice finally breaking. "Then you will spend your life in combat," she said. "Is that what you desire? Must every cruel word be answered with a pistol? When will it suffice?"

For a moment, his iron resolve faltered. He moved nearer to her, his voice sinking to a ragged whisper. "If I do not go," he said, "I will never be at peace with myself."

Rachel's tears finally fell, carving wet tracks through the lamplight. When she spoke, her voice was low and wounded. "Goodbye."

She turned and walked out of the room. Her footsteps echoed down the hall, each one cutting deeper than the last into the silence of the cabin. Jackson stood there, staring at the empty doorway long after she was gone. Slowly, he turned back to the desk and sank into his chair. His eyes drifted once more to the pistol as the candle flickered, casting long, dancing shadows against the log walls.

Buzzards

The following morning, a carriage jolted along an uneven dirt road. Inside, Charles Dickinson sat across from Hanson Catlet, looking relaxed and composed — every inch the man who believed the outcome of the next dawn was already predetermined. Catlet, by contrast, looked tight with nerves.

"Have you given any thought to an accommodation with the General?" Catlet asked, his voice barely rising above the rumble of the wheels. "A word of regret, perhaps, at least for what was said of his wife."

Dickinson scoffed, the sound sharp in the cramped cabin. "Have you ever known a man quicker with a pistol than I?"

Catlet shook his head. He turned to the window for a moment, watching the blurred trees pass, then looked back at his friend. "Jackson is stubborn as the Devil," he said, "and harder than most men you'll ever meet. He has stood before a cocked pistol more than once and never shown so much as a tremor. A man of that sort is not to be treated lightly."

"I have never lost an affair of honor, Hanson. You were present in Caroline County when that Irishman cursed me and demanded satisfaction." Dickinson snapped his hand up suddenly, mimicking the pistol and aiming it straight at Catlet's chest. He laughed, blowing invisible smoke from his index finger. "He did not live long enough to return fire."

Catlet grimaced but gave a slow, reluctant nod.

"Every man who has faced me has gone down,"

Dickinson went on, his voice dropping into a cold, confident register. "I see no reason this should prove otherwise." He leaned forward, locking eyes with Catlet. "One shot," he said quietly. "Decisive. Clean."

Catlet shifted uncomfortably on the leather seat, an edge of urgency creeping into his tone. "Charles, hear me. This need not end in blood. You could delope. Discharge your pistol and give the field its due without taking a life."

Dickinson's smirk vanished instantly, his eyes narrowing into slits. "Delope? And allow him to walk away after what he has said? After he has dragged my family into his filth?"

"I think," Catlet replied, "that a man with a wife, and a child soon to be born, has more before him than the satisfaction of a single moment."

Dickinson leaned back, shaking his head. "You do not understand. If I yield now, what follows me thereafter? That Charles Dickinson shrank from the field? That his honor failed him?"

Catlet's voice rose despite himself, his frustration boiling over. "And what comfort will honor be to you in the grave?" he demanded. "Think of Jane. Think of the child she carries. In a few short months, you should be holding your son or your daughter in your arms."

"In a few short months," Dickinson shot back, "I'll be known as the man who pruned this society of its most poisonous weed, and the most successful attorney in Nashville!"

Catlet fell silent. The steady, rhythmic rumble of the carriage wheels filled the space between them, underscoring the grim inevitability that Dickinson seemed to welcome. Catlet leaned forward one last time, his face a mask of concern. "Charles, I ask you as a friend."

Dickinson didn't answer right away. He stared out the window at the passing fields, his jaw set as he considered the plea. Then he turned back, his confidence fully restored. "Hanson, I do not doubt your regard," he said. "But my course is fixed. This will be decided tomorrow and Jackson will not leave the field."

Catlet sighed and leaned back, the resignation written plainly across his face. Suddenly, Dickinson's head snapped toward the window.

"Pull up," he said sharply. "Here, stop here."

The carriage slowed to a halt. Dickinson stepped down into the tall grass, Catlet following him, intrigued despite his own better judgment. Without hesitation, Dickinson raised his pistol toward a high tree limb where two squirrels sat. A sharp crack split the morning air, and the first squirrel dropped. The second darted down the branch, but another shot followed instantly. It fell beside the first.

Dickinson turned to Catlet with a smirk. Just then, a third squirrel burst from behind the trunk. Dickinson snapped his arm up and fired a third time. The squirrel dropped instantly. He turned slowly toward his second, measuring the effect of the display. "May I have your coat?"

Catlet blinked, his brow furrowing as he slipped the garment off. "My coat?"

"Think nothing of it," Dickinson said lightly. "You shall have another."

He took the coat and walked to a low-hanging branch, draping it neatly over the wood. With a practiced, lethal eye, he adjusted a secondary branch so that the right sleeve hung raised and the breast pocket faced outward like a target. He paced backward as he counted softly under his breath. When he reached twenty paces, he turned.

"Count me down," he said, drawing his second pistol.

Catlet hesitated, his stomach turning at the cold-bloodedness of the drill, but Dickinson was already poised. Reluctantly, Catlet spoke. "Five… four… three… two… one… fire."

Dickinson snapped his arm up. The shot was clean and sharp, the ball tearing a hole straight through the coat pocket. He let out a short, almost giddy laugh. He hurried forward, thrusting a finger through the hole in the fabric, and chuckled to himself as if admiring a clever parlor trick.

Catlet stared at the coat, unmistakably impressed despite the dread pooling in his gut.

"Come, Hanson," Dickinson said, his spirits high. "Back to the carriage."

Catlet followed without a word as they climbed back inside, the silence of the woods returning as the carriage rolled on toward Kentucky.

An hour later, a different carriage rolled gently along the same narrow dirt path. The countryside had grown quiet. Ahead, several buzzards circled lazily in the high, pale sky, marking something in the brush.

The carriage moved on for a few moments before Thomas Overton leaned forward as he pointed out the window. "Do you see it?"

Jackson straightened, his blue eyes piercing as he peered out. "A coat... a fine one." He leaned forward and called to the driver, his voice rasping. "Pull up here." The carriage slowed to a stop. Jackson and Thomas stepped down into the road. Overton moved closer to the dark object hanging limp from a low branch.

"There is a hole clean through the pocket," Thomas said, his fingers grazing the scorched wool. "As though a ball had passed straight through."

Jackson exhaled a sharp, cold breath. "He means to provoke me. A calling card."

A short distance away, a buzzard tore at something in the tall grass. Overton raised an eyebrow and scanned the area. "Andrew, look..."

A squirrel lay nearby, its head gone. Two more were visible beyond it, each executed with the same terrifying precision. Thomas's eyes widened.

Jackson took it in without a single word. Whatever flicker of concern stirred in his chest, he buried it beneath a layer of iron. He shook his head once and turned back toward the carriage. Thomas followed.
As the carriage resumed its journey, the two men passed the time in low, urgent conversation.

"Have you considered what my brother said?" Thomas asked, leaning in. "There is still a way to avoid bloodshed. If Mr. Dickinson's second can be brought to delope, and you will agree to do the same…"

Jackson sighed, staring straight ahead at the rhythmic bobbing of the horses' heads. "We will proceed as agreed."

Thomas hesitated. "How steady are you with a pistol, Andrew?"

"I am no great marksman," Jackson replied with a blunt honesty that chilled the air. "But I can shoot."

"I spoke with Coffee," Thomas said. "At the City Hotel they are laying wagers on the duel. Most of the money is on Dickinson. The boy himself has staked four hundred dollars over at Winn's."

Jackson looked at him, his expression unreadable. "There is more," he prompted.

"Coffee knows Dickinson's second, Mr. Catlet," Thomas went on, choosing his words with agonizing care. "He says Dickinson has been in several affairs of honor. He has never been beaten. And in each, the other man never managed to return fire."

"What?" Jackson said, the news finally catching him off guard. A rare flicker of surprise crossed his face.

Thomas continued, pressing the advantage of the moment. "Coffee has proposed something, though I do not know that you will entertain it."

"Say it."

"He believes you should wear my coat." Jackson glanced at him, confused. "You are tall, but I am the larger man," Thomas explained. "When Dickinson fires at you, he will be offered a broader mark, while your true frame is somewhat concealed. If the ball should strike, it may take cloth and wadding rather than flesh."

Jackson considered the notion for a second, the tactical logic of it appealing to his soldier's mind. "It is not a poor notion."

Thomas nodded, then hesitated, the most dangerous part of the plan still unsaid. "But there is more," he said. "And you may think it improper."

Jackson waited in a stony silence.

"What if you allow him to shoot first?"

Jackson looked at Thomas as though his friend had suddenly gone mad.

"Hear me," Thomas insisted, his words coming faster now. "When the word is given, he will draw and fire with speed. You will do the same. But if you miss, it is over. You will have had your chance."

"It is folly," Jackson snapped.

"You said yourself you are no great marksman," Thomas countered. "But with a moment to take aim, to be steady and deliberate, you could fell him. If you take his fire and stand your ground, the second shot is yours. He will have to stand there and wait for it."

Jackson said nothing for a long, agonizing minute. The idea of standing still and inviting a bullet from an expert marksman was a gamble with death itself.

"We have a long ride before us," he said at last. "I will consider it."

Thomas lowered his voice one last time, a final plea for his friend's life. "There is still the matter of deloping. You could both leave the field alive."

Jackson's restraint finally broke. "Thomas, deloping will not serve," he said sharply. "I will take my fire." He fixed Thomas with a look of cold, predatory finality. "That boy is not going back home."

Thomas fell silent and looked away out the window, the carriage rolling inexorably on toward the Red River.

"Fire!"

May 30, 1806, Logan County, Kentucky

The morning of the duel came too quickly. Jackson had not slept, not really. His body was worn down by the long, restless night, but his mind was sharp and alive with a fierce, unsettling clarity.

The first grey light of dawn crept through the cracks in the shutters of Jackson's room at the inn. The General knelt beside the bed, his head bowed. The room was silent except for the low, rhythmic murmur of his voice. A single dueling pistol lay on the pillow above him, its dark steel catching the faint light.

"And grant me thy protection from my enemy," he prayed softly, his voice a rasp in the quiet. "And give me the strength to persevere. Let thy will be done. Amen."

He remained on his knees for a long moment after the words left him, the gravity of what lay ahead pressing down on his shoulders like a physical stone. Then, slowly, he rose.

The door creaked faintly. Thomas Overton stood in the doorway, having stopped short when he realized what he was witnessing. He felt like an intruder, a man accidentally watching his friend make his final peace with his Maker. Jackson turned. Their eyes met. Thomas's were clouded with a visible, aching worry; Jackson's were hard and steady, lit with a predatory resolve.

"Good morning," Overton said quietly, the words feeling small in the heavy air.

Jackson nodded, and for a fleeting second, the severity in his face softened into something resembling a ghost of a smile. "Good morning, Thomas."

Overton glanced down at the oversized coat draped over his arm. It was broad, far too large for Jackson's slender frame. He hesitated, then held it out like a ceremonial robe. "Have you fully considered it?" he asked, his voice wavering. "There remains time to…"

"It's already done," Jackson said, his tone quiet but as firm as a slammed door.

He took the coat and slipped it on, adjusting the heavy wool with meticulous care. Thomas watched him, searching every line of his face for a sign of doubt or a tremor of the hand. He found neither.

"I saw you praying," Overton said.

Jackson paused, his hands stilling on the lapels of the coat. He looked at Thomas with an intensity that carried both a rare vulnerability and an unbreakable iron resolve. "A man should always make his peace with the Lord before battle."

Overton swallowed hard, the lump in his throat refusing to move. He stepped aside as Jackson moved toward the door with a measured, rhythmic stride.

"Come," Jackson said, his eyes already fixed on the horizon. "It is time."

Together, they stepped out into the pale, cold morning light, their boots crunching on the damp earth as they walked toward the Red River.

Forty miles away, back in Tennessee, the large log cabin was wrapped in a profound morning stillness.

Rachel Jackson sat alone at the heavy wooden table, the only sound the rhythmic, dry whisper of thin paper as she slowly turned the pages of the family Bible. Her lips moved silently, reciting verses under her breath. At last, her hand stopped. She placed both palms flat against the open pages, as if trying to draw strength directly from the ink, and bowed her head.

"Dear Lord," she whispered, her voice barely a thread in the quiet room. "Keep him in Your care. Watch his steps, steady his hand, and bring him home to me."

Her voice faltered, cracking on the last word. She drew a jagged breath, her eyes squeezed shut as she pressed back the tears that threatened to rise and break her resolve.

"You know the hardness of this world," she said softly, speaking to the empty room as if to a confidant. "And You know his nature."

She bowed her head lower.

"I ask no more than this, please, let him return."

Rachel lifted her head and looked out the window. The garden beyond was a lush, vibrant green, peaceful and indifferent in the early light. She watched the shadows retreat across the grass, praying with a desperate, quiet fervency that peace might somehow reach Andrew where she could not.

Back in Kentucky, the sun was high and the morning was bright and clear, the kind of spring day that felt almost indecent given where they were headed. Jackson's carriage rolled steadily toward the banks of the Red River, the rhythmic jolting of the wheels the only clock marking their final minutes.

Inside, Thomas Overton shifted uneasily on the leather seat. He wanted to speak, needed to, but nothing seemed right. Jackson sat opposite him, rigid and unmoving, staring out the window as the lush green fields and budding trees slipped past. His face was a mask of unreadable iron.

The quiet dragged on, thick and suffocating, until Thomas finally forced the words out. "A fine day," he said, his voice sounding thin in the cramped carriage. "One could not ask for better weather."

Jackson turned his head and looked at him. His expression was flat, his eyes distant as if he were looking through Thomas at something far on the horizon. After a brief, chilling moment, he turned back to the window, his gaze returning to the passing countryside. The silence closed in again, heavier and colder than before.

A short time later, Harrison's Mill and the winding silver of the river came into view.

Uncle Bob stood beside a carriage some distance from the dueling ground, waiting in the tall grass. Jackson's carriage rolled in and came to a stop, kicking up a fine veil of dust. Jackson stepped down first, his dueling pistol held firmly in hand, his face set with a singular, lethal purpose. Thomas Overton followed close behind, his boots heavy on the damp earth.

Uncle Bob approached them. For just a moment, Jackson's hard expression cracked, and a brief, ghost of a smile escaped him.

"General Jackson. It is always a pleasure, sir."

"Good morning, Bob."

They shook hands, a brief touch of humanity before the business at hand. "I saw what was printed in the paper," Uncle Bob said carefully, his voice lowered. "I can well understand why you have come."

Jackson said nothing.

"Sir…" Uncle Bob hesitated, suddenly aware of how precarious his position was, caught between two forces of nature. "He is a remarkable shot," he said at last. "I have seen him with a pistol." His voice dropped to a near whisper. "Perhaps there is still time for words. A meeting… You might both return home."

Jackson didn't answer. His eyes had already drifted past Bob to the far end of the field, where Hanson Catlet stood beside the silhouette of Charles Dickinson. Catlet broke away from his principal and began the long, measured walk toward them across the meadow.

"I shall go speak with him," Thomas Overton said, his voice tight with the realization that the talking was nearly over.

Jackson gave a short, sharp nod. Uncle Bob quietly retreated, disappearing toward the horses, leaving the General standing alone in the center of the bright, indifferent morning.

Jackson looked down at the oversized coat and began fastening the buttons. The fabric hung loosely on his lean frame, creating a deceptive silhouette.

Overton's nerves were plain as he walked out to meet Catlet in the center of the clearing. The grass was still damp with dew, clutching at their boots as the two men shook hands.

"Good morning, sir. I trust you had safe travels."

"Yes, yes," Overton replied, his voice a fraction too high. "I confess I have never stood as a second before. I suppose we must speak to the arrangements."

"I have stood with Mr. Dickinson in other affairs of honor in Maryland."

"Yes," Overton said faintly. "Other affairs."

Catlet did not soften the blow. "On each occasion, Mr. Dickinson was victorious."

Overton felt the weight of that statement settle heavily in his chest, a cold pressure that made it hard to draw a full breath.

"These affairs are never pleasant," Catlet went on. "I had hoped the General might choose to delope. If that is his wish, I will put the question to Mr. Dickinson."

"The General is resolved to proceed as settled," Overton said, finding a spark of firmness. "He will not throw away his shot."

Catlet's lingering hope for peace faded from his eyes. "Very well. Please come with me."

They walked to the middle of the field. Catlet pointed to the trampled grass at their feet. "Eight paces. Will that suffice?"

Overton hesitated, glancing back toward Jackson, who watched from a distance like a silent, waiting hawk. Reluctantly, he nodded. "It will."

"Then stand with your back to me and take twelve steps."

They turned back to back and walked the distance. Catlet removed a small piece of wood from his pocket and marked his spot. "Remain there." He crossed the distance and marked the opposite position. "These marks will be the location for Mr. Dickinson and the General,"

Catlet said. "I will toss for the word."

He reached into his pocket and pulled out a coin. "Head or tail?"

"Tail."

Catlet flipped the coin; it caught the morning sun in a silver flash before he caught it. "Tail it is," Catlet said. "You will give the word." Catlet leaned in closer, his voice dropping. "You will have heard of Mr. McNairy's quarrel with Mr. Coffee. A shot was fired before the signal."

Overton nodded, his uncertainty growing.

"Mr. Dickinson asks this," Catlet continued. "If either man fires before the word is given, the other shall be allowed his fire without reply. And if one is struck before the command and rendered unable, then you or I must discharge the pistol in his place."

Catlet held his gaze, the gravity of the pact hanging between them. "Is that understood?"

Overton swallowed hard. He had come to settle distances and words, not to imagine himself having to take up a pistol and kill a man. "If the General is prepared," Catlet said at last, "we may proceed."

Overton turned and walked back toward Jackson.

"You have done well," Jackson said calmly, his voice as steady as if they were discussing the weather.

Overton drew a jagged breath. "I will give the word to fire," he said, forcing the words out. "I beg you, do not discharge before the signal."

Jackson let out a short, dry chuckle. "We have already settled this," he said. "I will not raise my pistol until after he fires." He looked ahead, toward Dickinson. "And he will miss."

Overton managed a nervous, trembling smile.

"We may proceed," Jackson said. He extended his hand. Overton took it, holding on longer than he should have, his fingers gripping Jackson's as tears welled in his eyes.

"This way."

Jackson turned and walked toward the field. Overton followed a step behind, his heart hammering against his ribs. "Your mark is here."

Jackson spotted the small piece of wood and moved to it without hesitation. Across the field, Dickinson stepped to his own mark. Overton and Catlet retreated to the side, leaving the two combatants to face one another, locked in a silent, predatory glare.

"Gentlemen," Catlet called out. "Present your pistols downward."

Both men complied, the barrels pointing toward the grass.

"Mr. Overton will count from three to one and then give the word," Catlet continued, reciting the lethal liturgy of the *Code Duello*. "At the command, you will raise your pistols and fire. No shot is to be discharged before the signal." He paused, his eyes moving between the two rivals. "Are we understood?"

Dickinson gave a sharp, confident nod. Jackson never broke eye contact, his gaze as fixed and cold as the steel in his hand.

A heavy silence followed. The very air in the river bottom seemed to hold its breath; the birds had fallen silent, and the wind had died, as if the field itself were waiting for the violence to come.

"When you are ready, sir," Catlet said quietly to Overton, "you may give the count."

Overton drew a deep breath. His hand trembled

visibly as he raised it to signal the start. He looked at Jackson one last time, searching for a sign, a plea, or a prayer. Jackson merely met his gaze and gave a single, imperceptible nod.

"Three!"

Dickinson had been living for this exact second. His grip tightened around the wood of the pistol grip, his index finger twitching with anticipation.

"Two!"

A cold, unnatural stillness settled over Jackson. It was as if ice were running through his veins, freezing his posture into a permanent, unyielding mark.

"One!"

Overton whispered a final, silent prayer. For a single heartbeat, time seemed to grind to a halt.

"Fire!"

Dickinson moved with astonishing, predatory speed. His arm snapped upward in a blur of motion, and his pistol discharged with a sharp, violent crack that echoed off the trees. A thick plume of white sulfurous smoke bloomed around him, obscuring his view.

Jackson did not move.

He stood rigid, his eyes still locked forward, appearing for all the world like a statue emerging from the drifting haze. He didn't even flinch at the sound of the ball passing.

"Great God, have I missed?"

Dickinson's voice was high and panicked. He looked wildly toward Catlet for some confirmation of the impossible. Catlet stared back, utterly stunned. Confused and desperate, Dickinson stepped forward, his eyes scanning Jackson's oversized coat for the dark bloom of blood he knew should be there.

Overton surged forward, his voice a roar of authority. "Sir! You must remain at your mark!"

Catlet rushed in, physically grabbing Dickinson's arm to haul him back to the wooden stake. "Charles, get back!"

"He did not fire, did he?" Dickinson asked, his voice tightening into a knot of sheer terror.

"No," Catlet said, his voice hollow.

The realization struck Dickinson all at once, a physical weight that drained the color from his face. He understood now with terrifying clarity what came next.

Jackson, momentarily dazed by the shock of the impact, gathered himself. The field grew impossibly quiet, the silence more deafening than the gunshot had been. Dickinson could no longer keep still; he shifted and fidgeted, his boots scuffing the dirt as he instinctively tried to step away from the line of fire.

"Sir, please, to your mark!" Overton shouted.

Catlet's face fell as he realized the depth of the disaster. "The rules must be observed," he murmured, more to himself than anyone else. "The General is now entitled to his fire."

Jackson fixed his eyes on his rival. Dickinson forced himself to stand still, though his hands were trembling uncontrollably at his sides and his breath was coming in shallow, ragged gasps. Catlet took an involuntary, desperate step toward Jackson.

"General, do you wish to delope?"

Jackson's eyes flicked to the second, cold and unyielding.

"Sir..." Catlet said, his voice dropping to a plea.

For a heartbeat, Jackson appeared to hesitate. Then his attention returned to Dickinson, who was visibly unravelling before him. Without a word, Jackson slowly, deliberately raised his pistol.

Catlet backed away in sudden alarm. Jackson's hand was as steady as the horizon; his resolve did not waver for an instant. He squeezed the trigger.

Click.

The hammer fell, but the powder did not ignite. The pistol had misfired.

Jackson froze, caught completely off guard. Overton rushed toward Jackson in alarm, his eyes darting between the General and the unignited pistol.

"Is it settled?" Dickinson's voice cracked, the question trembling with a frantic, desperate hope. He looked to Catlet for an answer, for a reprieve, but Catlet had none to give.

Jackson didn't speak. With a terrifying, mechanical calm, he worked the hammer of the pistol, resetting the mechanism. He raised the weapon again. There was no hesitation.

BANG!

The shot roared across the open field, the sound a final, violent period to the dispute. Smoke billowed in a thick cloud. Dickinson staggered backward, his hands instinctively clutching his chest. His legs buckled beneath him, and he collapsed into the grass.

"Charles!" Catlet screamed, racing toward his fallen friend.

Dickinson lay on the ground, one hand pressed firmly against the blooming red stain on his shirt. He gasped, a wet, rattling cough forcing a spray of blood from his mouth. His breathing grew shallow and uneven, each ragged breath coming with significantly greater effort than the last.

Across the field, Jackson's triumph was cut short by a sudden, searing pain that tore through his chest. He staggered, clutching his side as the adrenaline began to fade and the shock set in. His face tightened into a mask of agony.

"Andrew, are you wounded?" Overton called out, rushing to his side.

Jackson tried to speak, but the words were barely a rasp. "I am not hurt," he said softly, the lie failing even as he spoke it.

Then his knees gave way. He dropped to the ground, and Overton was there instantly, gripping his arm to keep him upright. "You have been struck," Overton said urgently. "You must be tended to at once."

Jackson braced himself, the old soldier refusing to show weakness even as the world tilted. He did not resist as Overton helped him back to his feet. Together, they moved slowly toward the carriage.

Behind them, Catlet knelt in the dirt, his hands slick with blood as he cradled Dickinson. "Charles... Charles..."

Dickinson coughed again, his eyes fluttering. "Did my ball strike him?" he gasped.

Catlet swallowed hard, his voice breaking with a mercy that cost him dearly. "You did. You met him honorably."

A carriage pulled up nearby. Uncle Bob jumped down, his face draining of color at the sight of the fallen man. "Oh no..."

Uncle Bob and Catlet lifted Dickinson's limp body into the carriage. Catlet climbed in after him, his clothes already ruined. "Go, Bob, go!" he shouted.

The carriage lurched forward. As it gathered

speed, the road grew rougher, every rut and stone sending a fresh jolt through Dickinson's shattered body. He cried out, then screamed, the sound raw and unrestrained, echoing through the trees. Catlet pressed his hands to the wound, trying in vain to slow the relentless bleeding.

"You are wounded," Catlet said, his voice shaking. "We must act quickly."

The carriage rattled on until a building finally came into view. The horses slowed and stopped. Uncle Bob leapt down and flung the door open. "Charles," he said, his voice trembling. "We are going to tend to you. Stay with us."

Dickinson answered only with a low, hollow moan.

Catlet and Bob half-carried, half-dragged Dickinson inside. They burst through the door, leaving a trail of crimson staining the floorboards behind them. "We need a bed!"

A young woman in the hallway froze at the sight of the gore, her hand flying to her mouth in horror. Without a word, she pointed down the hall. They rushed into the room and laid Dickinson on the bed. Bob hovered helplessly by the door. "What shall I do?"

"Stand back," Catlet commanded.

Dickinson lay pale and clammy by the window, the white sheets beneath him quickly soaking through with crimson. Catlet leaned over him, his clinical composure finally shattering. "I apologize," he said quietly. "This will be painful."

He plunged his fingers into the entry wound.

Dickinson writhed and shrieked in agony as Catlet searched inside him, his fingers probing desperately for the ball. Uncle Bob stood nearby, his face twisted with an anguish that mirrored the dying man's.

"The ball is lodged too deep," Catlet said grimly, withdrawing his hands. "I cannot reach it."

Bob grabbed Dickinson's hand and held on with a crushing grip as Catlet tried one last time. "Charles," Catlet urged. "Hold fast. You must keep with us."

At last, Catlet withdrew. Dickinson's breathing had grown shallow and uneven. His eyes flickered open and found Catlet's face. "Hanson... tell Jane..." he whispered.

Catlet shook his head, tears finally spilling over. "No, you will tell her. Stay with me."

Dickinson's gaze drifted upward toward the ceiling. His voice was barely a breath, a final question to the universe. "Who put out the lights?"

Catlet's face crumpled as the last spark of life slipped from his friend. Dickinson's hand went slack in Uncle Bob's grasp. The room fell into a terrifying, absolute silence. Uncle Bob bowed over the bed and began to cry.

Catlet stood there, staring at the blood-soaked sheets. He lowered his head, stunned and broken.

Charles Dickinson was dead.

◆ ◆ ◆ ◆ ◆ ◆

A few miles away, a small tavern hummed with midday chatter.

The door pushed open, and Thomas Overton stepped inside, half-carrying Jackson. The General was pale but remained upright. He reached out, gripping the edge of a table for balance, before lowering himself into a chair with an involuntary wince. Overton hovered close, his eyes darting across the room in a frantic scan for help.

"Barkeep!" he shouted.

The barkeep hurried over, his smile vanishing as he saw the dark, spreading stain of blood seeping through Jackson's linen shirt. "Sir, are you injured?"

Jackson waved him off with a grimace. "Two whiskeys," he rasped. "Quickly."

The barkeep hesitated for a heartbeat, then disappeared behind the bar. Overton leaned down, his voice a tight, urgent whisper. "We must have you seen to, Andrew. This is no small thing."

Jackson shifted in the chair, a fresh flare of pain crossing his face, but his expression remained unnervingly calm. "Let it be for a moment, Thomas," he said quietly. "Just a moment of peace."

The barkeep returned and set two glasses on the table. Jackson lifted one with a hand that trembled despite his will, but he managed a stoic, bloody smile as he caught Overton's eye.

"To victory."

Overton shook his head, exhaling a breath that was half-frustration and half-shattered admiration. Jackson took a sip, closing his eyes to savor the familiar burn. As he did, Overton's eyes dropped to the floor. A dark, pool of blood was forming beneath Jackson's left boot.

"Andrew…"

Jackson followed the look and lifted his pant leg. Blood was dripping steadily, rhythmically, into his shoe.

"That settles it," Overton said, his voice brooking no further argument. "We are finding a doctor." He motioned to the barkeep, who pointed toward a disheveled man slumped in a corner, nursing a drink.

"That's Jeremiah Majors," the barkeep said. "He studied medicine."

Overton crossed the room without hesitation. "Sir, my friend's been shot. Can you tend to him?"

Majors looked up, his eyes bleary but mildly amused. "That fellow?" he said, gesturing toward the table. "The one smiling as though fortune itself had shaken his hand?"

"Yes," Overton replied tightly. "It has been a trying morning."

Majors chuckled as he stood. "Very well," he said. "Let us see what trouble he has brought with him."

In the back room, Majors swept a clutter of plates and glasses off a table and gestured for Jackson to sit. "Off with the coat and shirt. Let's have a look."

Jackson complied as he shrugged out of the heavy, blood-soaked fabric. Majors examined the puckered wound, then shot a significant glance at Overton.

"Another drink," Majors said. "He will need it. This will not be gentle."

Overton hurried out and returned with two fresh glasses. He pressed one into Jackson's hand. "Drink."

Jackson downed it in a single, practiced motion. Majors began probing the wound. Jackson's face tightened but he didn't make a single sound.

"The fortunate part," Majors said, leaning back slightly, "is that the ball has missed anything vital. An inch to the right and you'd be meeting your Maker."

Overton stared at him, scarcely breathing.

"The misfortune," Majors continued, "is that it lies buried deep against the bone."

"Can you remove it?" Overton asked.

Majors hesitated, looking at his limited tools. "I may attempt it. But it will hurt more than the shot itself."

"Do it," Jackson said through clenched teeth.

Majors went to work. Jackson gripped the edge of the table until his knuckles turned white, the pain ripping through him—but he stayed silent. Finally, Majors stepped back and wiped his hands on a rag.

"I could not reach it," he said flatly. "But I believe you will live. That heavy coat likely spared you; it took the main force from the ball before it hit your skin."

Overton let out a long, shuddering breath and handed Jackson another drink. "You must watch it closely," Majors warned.

"I will see him to his own physician in Nashville," Overton replied.

Jackson took a cautious sip of the whiskey. "Thomas," he said, his voice returning to its usual gravelly strength, "I have endured worse."

Overton shook his head, looking at his friend's chest. "You are fortunate to be alive, General." He turned toward the door. "I am going to fetch another whiskey."

"I require no more, Thomas," Jackson said, thinking his second was concerned for him.

Overton smirked. "No. This one is for me."

Jackson laughed—a sudden, sharp sound that quickly turned into a racking cough. The sound echoed through the small back room as the reality of the day finally began to catch up with him.

"From Dust We Came"

That night, Uncle Bob drove the carriage hard toward Peach Bottom. His hands were tight on the reins, his mind racing even faster than the wheels. Ploughboy hadn't been running right; Bob had heard it in the gait, a slight, nagging unevenness in the stride, and he'd had the horse reshod. If he'd simply let Erwin take the horse to the track, win or lose, none of this would have happened. Charles Dickinson wouldn't be dead.

A soft, strangled sound rose from the carriage behind him. Sniffling. Bob didn't turn; he couldn't bring himself to look. "Dr. Catlet," he called back, his voice strained, "we're near the house."

Inside the carriage, Hanson Catlet sat hunched and hollow-eyed, grief grinding him down in the dark. At his feet, Charles Dickinson's body lay crumpled on the floorboards, his legs bent awkwardly and his coat darkened with blood that had already turned into a tacky, iron-scented stain. When the wheels rattled over a deep rut, the body shifted. Catlet flinched as if the dead man were still alive.

Peach Bottom finally came into view, still and sleeping, its windows dark and unsuspecting. The carriage slowed to a crawl before rolling to a stop at the front steps. Inside, the mansion stood silent, holding the night at bay. The parlor was lit by a single oil lamp, its weak flame flickering against the polished wooden walls where Joseph Erwin sat motionless in a large armchair, staring into the dying embers of the fireplace. The silence was heavy, oppressive.

A sharp knock at the door broke the spell. Erwin

stiffened as Uncle Bob entered. His clothes were smeared with dark, drying blood, and he stopped just inside the threshold as if unsure he was even allowed to stand on the rug. His face told the entire story before he ever opened his mouth. He started to speak, closed his mouth, and then finally managed, "Mr. Catlet wishes to speak to you."

Erwin rose slowly, his voice a whisper. "Where is Charles?"

Bob swallowed hard. "Mr. Catlet is here. It's urgent."

Erwin nodded, dread tightening his chest like a physical weight. Bob stepped aside to let Catlet enter. The doctor held his hat in his hands, his fingers clutching the brim as if it were the only thing keeping him upright.

"Good evening, Mr. Erwin."

"Where's Charles?"

Catlet's lip trembled. He shook his head slowly. "I have just returned from the Red River."

Erwin's heart sank. "And?"

When Catlet only shook his head again, Erwin staggered back a step, gripping the arm of his chair to keep from falling. "No," he breathed. "No—that cannot be."

"The General's shot struck him in the chest," Catlet said, his voice breaking. "Charles did not survive."

The room went still, the air becoming suddenly thin and suffocating. Erwin collapsed back into his armchair and buried his face in his hands. Then, the sound of soft footsteps echoed in the doorway. Jane Dickinson stood there, her pregnancy unmistakable in the lamplight. Her face tightened as she took in the two men.

"Hanson? Father?" she asked. "Where's Charles?"

No one answered. Catlet looked at the floor. Erwin's eyes darted toward him, then away.

"Father?" Jane pressed, panic creeping into her voice. She stepped forward, one hand protectively cradling her belly. "Hanson, where's my husband?"

Catlet's mouth opened, but no words came. "Jane..." he began.

She froze. "No. No, do not say it. He... He went to Kentucky on business. He will return tomorrow." She turned to Hanson, searching his face with a desperate, frantic energy. "He will."

It was not a question, but a plea for a reality that no longer existed. Catlet's face twisted with regret. "Charles... he did not tell you. He did not go to Kentucky for business."

Jane stared at him, the truth sinking in like a stone dropped into deep water. "What are you saying?" Her knees buckled. Erwin rushed to steady her, but she pulled away with a sudden, violent strength. "Tell me where he is!"

Catlet looked away. "He went to meet General Jackson on the field."

Jane staggered back, her hand flying to her mouth. "A duel? No, no, he would not. He is to be a father!"

"He believed he was bound to it," Catlet said softly. "He thought he must answer what had been said, defend the family..."

"The family?" Jane cried, tears spilling freely now. "What of me? What of the child?" She collapsed into a chair, her voice turning hollow. "He lied to me. He looked me in the eye and swore he was going to Kentucky on business. He swore it!"

Her grief turned sharp as a blade, and she fixed her gaze on her father. "You knew. You knew, and you let him go."

Erwin's shoulders sagged as he wiped at his eyes. "I tried. He would not listen."

Jane shook her head, covering her face. "He should have been here. He should have been here with me."

"He met the General honorably," Catlet said, but the moment the word left his mouth, he knew it was worthless. Her sobs filled the room, jagged and raw. Catlet hesitated, then set his hat back upon his head. "Mr. Erwin… Jane… I am terribly sorry."

He turned and left the house. Erwin dropped to his knees beside his daughter, helpless as she wept. "Jane," he said softly, "I will see you and the child provided for. I give you my word."

She didn't respond. One hand rested over her belly, over the child who would never know its father. "He promised he would return," she whispered to the empty room.

The fire crackled softly, the only sound in the house besides the tears of a new widow.

♦♦♦♦♦♦

On the other side of Nashville, night hung heavy over the fields surrounding the log cabin near the Cumberland River. A carriage rolled up the dirt path, the rhythmic crunch of gravel the only sound in the quiet air, before coming to a halt.

Thomas Overton stepped down first. He turned back and offered his arm as Andrew Jackson descended with painstaking care. Jackson's face was ghostly, his movements slow and deliberate. He pressed a hand firmly to his side, wincing with each step, yet he forced his posture upright. Even wounded, his resolve remained a suit of armor.

The front door flew open, and Rachel appeared on the porch. Her eyes locked onto him instantly. She gasped at the sight of the blood-darkened cloth and the way he heavily favored his right side.

"Andrew!" she cried, hurrying toward him with her skirts trailing in the night breeze.

Jackson straightened as best he could, managed a faint, flickering smile as she reached him. "I am home, my love."

Rachel wrapped her arms around him without hesitation, holding him tightly despite the sharp spike of pain it caused him. Her tears spilled freely against his coat. "I thought… I thought I'd lost you."

Jackson gently eased her back just enough to brush her cheek with his hand. "It will take more than pistol and ball to part me from you," he said quietly.

Her sobs deepened as she shook her head, her voice thick with the exhaustion of the wait. "You owe nothing to anyone. I care nothing for what they say." She searched his face, her grip tightening on his sleeves. "Only promise me this… Promise you will not leave me so again."

Jackson hesitated. For a moment, the iron in his gaze softened, and tears gathered in his own eyes. He leaned forward and kissed her forehead, a tender gesture that pointedly avoided a promise he wasn't sure he could keep.

A short distance away, Thomas Overton watched in silence, leaning against the carriage to grant them what little privacy the yard afforded. Eventually, Rachel turned and went inside to prepare for his care. Jackson stayed behind a moment, glancing back at his friend.

"I will be along," he called softly.

Clutching his side, Jackson leaned his weight against a porch column. He watched Overton, who was preparing to depart. "Thomas."

Overton turned back. Jackson gestured him closer, and the second walked back toward the steps. "You have been a loyal friend," Jackson said.

"You would do the same for me."

Jackson let out a short, dry chuckle that ended in a grimace. "Thomas, I do not believe you are fool enough to cross state lines merely to stand still and be shot at by a practiced hand."

Overton smiled faintly. "On that point, General, I believe you are quite correct."

Jackson nodded, his mind already turning to the debts of the day. "About that coat of yours… I shall see to it you get a new one. A much finer one."

Overton let out a quiet laugh. "A fine coat will not keep me from trouble if I am in your company, General."

A faint grin tugged at the corner of Jackson's mouth. "Perhaps not. But you may as well be properly dressed for it."

A sudden, racking cough seized Jackson, and he pressed his hand tighter against the wound in his chest. Overton stepped forward, concerned. "You ought to be resting."

"Go on," Jackson wheezed, waving him off. "Get yourself home. You have done enough for one day."

He gave his friend a warm, tired smile. Overton climbed into the carriage, casting one last look back at the shadow of the man on the porch before the driver snapped the reins. Jackson watched the carriage until it disappeared into the blackness of the path.

Inside the cabin, the air was warmer, smelling of beeswax and herbs. He moved slowly down the hall, each step a victory over the lead ball in his chest.

"Andrew, come lie down," Rachel called from the bedroom.

"Yes, my love. I will be right there."

Before joining her, Jackson stepped into his study. He crossed to the heavy wooden desk and opened the top drawer. He removed the pistol from his coat and placed it inside. He shoved the drawer closed with a heavy thud of finality, turned his back on the room, and walked toward the light of the hallway.

◆◆◆◆◆◆

The following evening, the City Hotel hummed with a restless, frantic energy. Smoke from dozens of cigars hung like a low cloud over the tables, and every time the front door creaked open, the room fell into a momentary, breathless silence before the chatter resumed. No one knew the outcome of the duel yet, but everyone had an opinion and a stake.

John Overton sat at their usual table, his spine rigid. A glass of whiskey sat before him, a rare indulgence for the judge, whose nerves had finally frayed beyond his ability to maintain a calm demeanor. John Coffee sat opposite him, his injured leg stretched out awkwardly beneath the table. He watched Overton's hand tremble as he reached for the glass and let out a low, gravelly chuckle.

"Have you heard any word?" Coffee asked, his voice steady despite the mounting tension.

Overton merely shook his head, staring into the amber liquid as if it could tell him whether his best friend was lying in a Kentucky field or headed home.

At the neighboring table, Thomas Benton and his brother Jesse leaned in close. Catching the heavy silence at the General's table, Thomas tilted his head toward them. "I put ten dollars on the General," Thomas said. "The odds were good. Dickinson had the reputation but Jackson has never been quick to yield."

The front door swung open again. This time, the room didn't return to its chatter. Thomas Overton stepped inside, looking as though he had aged a decade in a single day. John Overton stood so abruptly his chair screeched against the floorboards. Coffee tried to move, but he shifted painfully, unable to get to his feet quickly due to the wound in his leg.

Thomas Overton scanned the room until he found them. He didn't speak at first, letting the silence hang. Then, a smile began to pull at the corners of his mouth—a small flicker that grew until it transformed his weary face.

"The General lives!" Thomas exclaimed.

John Overton rushed over and threw his arms around his brother, a rare public display of emotion that drew cheers from half the bar and groans from the men who had bet on Dickinson. At the table, Coffee knocked his fist loudly on the wood in a staccato of excitement, his face lit with a fierce, triumphant joy.

Thomas Benton's eyes widened. He looked to

Thomas Overton. "And Mr. Dickinson?"

Thomas Overton grimaced and dropped his gaze for a moment. When he looked back up, he met Benton's eyes and gave a slow, somber shake of his head.

Benton stood there for a moment, torn. He knew both men, if not well, then well enough to feel the weight of the news. Jesse rose first, breaking the spell. "Come along," he said. "Let's go to Winn's and get your money."

Benton gave Overton a brief, respectful nod, then followed Jesse to the door.

Thomas Overton looked to his brother, his voice raspy. "I need a drink."

As the two brothers moved to the bar, John Coffee gritted his teeth against the pull in his thigh and pushed himself to his feet. Leaning hard on his cane, he limped after them to join the celebration as a fresh round of whiskey slid down the counter.

♦♦♦♦♦♦

Two days later, Peach Blossom felt like a different world.

A heavy gray sky pressed low over the mansion, and a thin, persistent drizzle fell steadily, turning the yard dark and slick. The air was thick with the smell of wet earth and the sharp scent of woodsmoke from the kitchen fire. No birds chirped in the trees; even the dogs remained huddled under the shelter of the porch.

A wagon moved slowly across the grass, cutting shallow, muddy tracks into the soft ground. Resting in the bed was a pine coffin. Rain stippled the raw wood of the lid and ran down the sideboards in clear, shimmering lines.

Joseph Erwin walked behind it, his shoulders drawn, his face set in a mask of stunned exhaustion. Beside him was Jane pregnant, hollow-eyed, and ghostly pale. One hand was pressed protectively to her belly. She tried not to stare at the coffin.

She failed.

Every few steps, her gaze drifted back to the pine box. Erwin offered his arm once, quietly, without forcing the gesture, but she didn't take it. She walked as if she were made of glass.

Behind them trailed a small, somber cluster of mourners in black. A few umbrellas bobbed in the distance, but most had come without them, their coats darkening and their hats dripping with the rain. Uncle Bob followed with his head lowered. Thomas Swann walked a few paces behind, subdued now, his usual hunger for attention muted by the crushing loss of his friend.

The procession reached the family cemetery behind the mansion, a modest patch of ground bordered by a low fence and weeping trees, where a few large grave markers rose like sentinels among the smaller stones. The minister stepped forward, Bible in hand, and began to speak.

"From dust we came, and to dust we shall return. Let us commend the soul of Charles Dickinson into the hands of our Creator."

As he spoke, Jane's breathing grew shallow. Her hand stayed fixed at her belly, her palm pressing harder against the fabric of her dress as if feeling for movement—seeking proof that some part of her life still continued while another was being buried. The minister's words went on, offering comfort in practiced phrases.

Four men stepped forward. They lifted the coffin from the wagon and set it onto the heavy ropes. The wood creaked as the weight settled.

Jane flinched at the sound.

The coffin was lowered slowly, the wet ropes sliding through the men's hands. The box hovered for a heartbeat over the open earth, then sank into the dark rectangle of the grave. When it finally touched the bottom, something in Jane finally broke. She gripped the fence, her shoulders trembling as quiet, ragged sobs spilled free.

Erwin stepped closer and laid a gentle, tentative hand on her shoulder. His voice was barely a whisper. "He thought it was his duty."

Jane shook her head, refusing the hollow explanation.

Then came the sound that made everything real: the sound of wet dirt striking wood. One shovelful, then another, a dull, thudding rhythm that turned a man into a memory. Jane turned away, unable to watch the earth swallow him.

    Uncle Bob stepped forward and offered his arm. This time, she took it. He guided her back toward the mansion with a gentleness that spoke the words no one else could find.

    Erwin remained at the graveside a moment longer, staring at the fresh mound as the rain thickened and beaded on his wool coat. "Why didn't you listen?" he murmured.

    The drizzle became a steady fall. At last, he turned and followed the others, walking back toward the house as the grave disappeared behind the veil of the rain.

♦♦♦♦♦♦

    Twenty miles away, the same storm raged over the log cabin. Rain hammered the porch roof in a relentless, rhythmic drumming that nearly swallowed the slow, steady creak of Jackson's rocking chair. He sat facing the fields. A half-empty glass of whiskey rested on the railing beside him, the amber liquid jumping with every roll of thunder.

    Jackson rubbed absently at his chest, his fingers tracing the tender, inflamed skin where the lead ball still lay buried deep against his ribs. His face was a mask of unreadable iron, but his eyes carried the weight of everything he refused to say — and everything he could never take back.

    Behind him, the door groaned as Rachel appeared in the frame. She watched him in silence for a long moment as the storm began to lose its frantic strength.

The rain thinned to a drizzle, and the thunder began to roll farther away toward the horizon. When she finally stepped onto the porch, the damp, heavy air tugged at the hem of her dress.

"The storm's letting up," she said.

Jackson didn't look at her. His gaze remained fixed on the horizon. "It always does," he replied.

He took a measured sip of the whiskey, the burn a familiar comfort against the deeper ache in his side. The rocking chair creaked in the widening silence that followed.

"There will be other storms," Jackson said, his eyes narrowing as if seeing the years ahead. "Always."

Rachel sat in the chair beside him. A light, cooling drizzle still fell, and the air smelled richly of wet earth and rain-soaked cedar. She looked at him, her face etched with a plea that went beyond words.

"Promise me, Andrew," she said, her voice trembling. "No more dueling. No more blood."

Jackson hesitated. He slowly reached over and placed his hand over hers, a gesture of brittle reassurance.

"I will try," he said. The words were spoken so quietly they were almost lost to the wind.

Far off, a final jagged vein of lightning flickered one last time along the horizon. The fields shone faintly beneath the thinning clouds. Jackson leaned back into the chair, the rhythmic *creak-thud* of the wood blending with the last distant, dying roll of thunder.

He closed his eyes for a moment, the lead in his chest was a permanent reminder that while the honor was satisfied, there was no undoing what had been done on the banks of the Red River.

"Some Wounds"

January 29, 1835, Washington D.C.

Dr. Sneed sat on the edge of the large bed, momentarily speechless. In his short career as a physician in Washington, he had seen the toll of war and the ravages of age, but he had encountered nothing quite like the man before him.

"My God," Sneed said at last, his voice a low breath of disbelief. "It is incredible. It is a miracle you are still alive, sir."

Andrew Jackson gave a low, almost amused chuckle that turned into a raspy cough. He took a careful, measured sip of whiskey from the glass on his nightstand. The pain had never truly left him; it was a constant companion, a dull throb that anchored him to the earth. He shifted slightly against the propped-up pillows, searching for a position that might offer a moment's reprieve for his ravaged ribs.

"I survived," Jackson said, his voice like grinding gravel. "But some wounds... they do not leave a mark the eye can see."

His gaze drifted across the lamplit room to the corner where a portrait of Rachel hung. Her eyes seemed to follow him, filled with the same gentle spirit he had once tried to shield with a pistol. "The ball stays in the body, Doctor," Jackson said quietly, his hand resting near the old entry wound from the Red River. "But the words... they go for the heart."

Sneed followed the President's eyes to the portrait. Jackson remained silent for a long moment before he added, "My Rachel had a heart of gold. It did not hold."

Sneed nodded solemnly. He knew the history, the resurrected scandal of her first marriage dragged back into the mud during the brutal campaigns. Jackson's eyes, usually clouded with age, hardened into blue flint. "They said things," he murmured, the old fire flickering. "Printed them. She carried the shame of their lies until she couldn't."

Jackson leaned back, the flickering lamplight catching the accumulated marks of a life spent courting danger and defying the inevitable. "It has been settled," he said, though his tone suggested the cost had been higher than any man should pay.

The door opened softly, and Sarah Jackson stepped into the room. she paused, her eyes darting between the physician and the President with a protective sharp-sightedness. "How is he, Doctor?"

Sneed rose from his chair, smoothing his coat. "He is well enough, Mrs. Jackson. The ball gives him some discomfort, as it always will. I may offer something for the pain, yet there is truly nothing else to be done."

"There is an engagement at the Capitol in the morning," Sarah said, turning her attention to Jackson. "You should try to rest."

A low, heavy rumble passed through the house—distant, but unmistakable. Sneed turned toward the sound as Jackson shifted under a quilt. "It sounds as though a storm is coming on," the President noted, his eyes narrowing as if recognizing an old enemy.

"Then you should take your rest, Mr. President," Sneed urged.

As the doctor stood to leave, Jackson moved to adjust his position, and the sleeve of his nightshirt slipped. Sneed caught sight of another jagged, silvered scar running along the President's left arm.

"Sir," Sneed said gently, his professional curiosity getting the better of him. "Your arm… what happened there?"

Jackson followed the doctor's eyes and smiled faintly, a look of grim recognition as if he were greeting a troublesome old acquaintance. "Old business in Nashville."

Sneed waited, sensing the ghosts of the past crowding the room. Jackson glanced down at the scar, his thumb tracing the line of the old wound. "The Bentons," he added.

Sneed frowned, searching his memory of Tennessee politics. "Jesse Benton?"

Jackson nodded slowly. "And his brother, Thomas Benton, Old Bullion." He said nothing more, merely watching the doctor as the realization slowly settled in.

"Wait… Thomas Benton…" Sneed's eyes widened. "The Senator from Missouri?"

Jackson's faint smile didn't waver. "We had a disagreement."

Sneed studied him a moment longer, realizing that the man before him was held together by sheer, unbreakable willpower as much as he was by flesh and bone. "Very well, Mr. President."

He stepped out and closed the door softly. Sneed stood in the hall for a heartbeat, listening to the rain begin to lash against the White House windows. Death had come for Andrew Jackson more than once, and each time, the General had turned it away—not through mercy, and certainly not through caution, but through a sheer, unyielding refusal to leave the field.

Author's Note

Rachel Jackson's marriage to Andrew Jackson was the subject of public scandal during his lifetime and was repeatedly used against him by political enemies like John Quincy Adams and Henry Clay.

When Rachel first became involved with Andrew Jackson, she believed herself to be legally divorced from her first husband, Lewis Robards. That belief was shared by Jackson and by others around her like John Overton. Only later did it become clear that Robards had not yet completed the legal process required to finalize the divorce. As a result, Rachel and Andrew's initial marriage was not legally valid.

Once the error was discovered and Robards's divorce was formally completed, Rachel and Andrew Jackson remarried legally in 1794. Despite this, accusations of adultery and bigamy followed Rachel for the rest of her life, resurfacing most viciously during Jackson's presidential campaigns.

There is no credible evidence that Rachel Jackson knowingly deceived Andrew Jackson or acted with intent to scandalize. Contemporary accounts and later historical research strongly suggest that she believed, in good faith, that she was free to remarry. The attacks on her character were political weapons, not reflections of her conduct.

Those accusations deeply wounded Andrew Jackson and played a significant role in shaping his personal code of honor, his readiness to answer insults with violence, and his enduring sense that the world was conspiring to humiliate his family.

Rachel Jackson died in 1828, shortly before Andrew

Jackson took office as President of the United States. Jackson blamed the stress and cruelty of the attacks against her by supporters of John Quincy Adams for hastening her death.

♦♦♦♦♦♦

The duel between Andrew Jackson and Charles Dickinson did not arise from a single insult, but from a long chain of personal, political, and social conflicts that spiraled beyond anyone's control.

Much of the hostility can be traced back to a violent confrontation between Andrew Jackson and attorney Thomas Swann. Swann had publicly insulted Jackson's wife, Rachel, repeating accusations that questioned the legitimacy of her marriage. Jackson confronted Swann, and the encounter escalated into a brutal physical beating. The incident deepened existing divisions among Nashville's political and legal circles and set off a series of retaliatory disputes.

One of those disputes involved Judge John McNairy and merchant Joseph Coffee. McNairy, the brother of Jackson's mentor, became embroiled in a quarrel with Coffee that culminated in a duel. During that encounter, McNairy fired prematurely, violating the agreed-upon rules of honor. In order to get around being shot by Coffee on the field, he penned a letter to a Nashville newspaper explaining what had happened.

Another critical catalyst of the Jackson-Dickinson duel was a horse race organized by Joseph Erwin. Horse racing in early Tennessee was not merely sport; it was a public test of reputation, wealth, and credibility. Disputes over the outcome of the race, particularly accusations of dishonesty and unpaid wagers, ignited further resentment. Harsh words followed, many of them printed in newspapers, where they could not be ignored or quietly resolved.

Charles Dickinson entered this volatile atmosphere already known as a skilled and dangerous duelist. Years before his clash with Andrew Jackson, Dickinson had participated in multiple affairs of honor in Maryland and Kentucky and had emerged undefeated. Contemporary accounts consistently described him as a fast and confident pistol shot, and in more than one encounter his opponent was struck before managing to return fire. That reputation followed him, lending real menace to his words.

When Dickinson publicly repeated and amplified insults against Andrew Jackson, especially those aimed at Rachel Jackson, the accumulated grievances finally converged. What might have been defused earlier now carried the weight of years of bruised pride and unresolved slights, sharpened by the knowledge that the man issuing the insults was widely believed to be lethal.

The Jackson–Dickinson duel was therefore not an isolated act of rash violence, but the inevitable result of a culture that treated reputation as currency and bloodshed as a legitimate means of defense. Each confrontation fed the next, until no participant could retreat without appearing to surrender honor itself.

Understanding this chain of events is essential to understanding Andrew Jackson, not as a man quick to violence for its own sake, but as one shaped by a world where public insult, political rivalry, and personal loyalty collided with lethal consequences.

The duel itself took place on May 30, 1806, along the Red River near the Tennessee-Kentucky border, a location chosen to avoid Tennessee's strict anti-dueling laws. The terms were severe. The two men would stand at close range, approximately eight paces, and fire at a single command. Unlike many affairs of honor, neither man agreed to delope by firing harmlessly into the air.

Dickinson, widely regarded as the faster and more accurate shot, fired first. His ball struck Andrew Jackson in the chest, lodging dangerously close to Jackson's heart. Jackson, though gravely wounded, remained standing. According to witnesses, he steadied himself, raised his pistol deliberately, and tried to fire. However, the gun misfired. Jackson re-cocked his pistol and fired. His shot struck Dickinson in the chest, inflicting a wound that proved fatal later that day.

Dickinson was carried from the field and died several hours afterward. Jackson, despite his injury, refused immediate medical aid and did not leave the ground until the formalities of the duel were complete. The ball that struck him could not be safely removed and remained lodged in his body for the rest of his life, a constant reminder of the encounter.

In the immediate aftermath, public reaction was divided. Some viewed Jackson's conduct as a chilling display of resolve; others condemned the duel as reckless and unnecessary. What was not disputed was the finality of the outcome. One man was dead. The other carried the wound—physically and morally for decades.

The duel ended the immediate chain of retaliation, but it did not end the controversy surrounding Andrew Jackson. Instead, it cemented his reputation as a man who would endure extraordinary pain rather than yield an inch of honor, a reputation that would follow him for the rest of his public life.

◆◆◆◆◆◆◆

According to Dickinson family lore, as Charles Dickinson lay dying after the duel, he gave instructions that his body be returned to his family's home in Caroline County, Maryland. The slave who accompanied him followed those instructions, placing Dickinson's remains in a lead coffin and beginning the journey, first back toward Nashville, and then onward to Maryland.

As the years passed and the community expanded, the place where Dickinson was said to rest slipped quietly from record and recollection.

More than a century later, in 1965, a lead coffin was discovered in a cornfield near the Dickinson family property in Maryland. Though initial excitement suggested the long-lost duelist had been found, a study of the remains revealed the bones were most likely those of a woman. Even so, the Caroline County Historical Society placed a marker at the site, identifying it as the presumed resting place of Charles Dickinson.

The matter might have ended there except that Dickinson's name returned to the newspapers, and with it, old questions resurfaced in Nashville.

Around that time, a woman living in West Nashville came forward with an unusual claim. The deed to her home on Carden Avenue, she said, made reference to a gravesite on the property—specifically, that of

Charles Dickinson. The house stood only a short walk from the former location of Joseph Erwin's Peach Blossom plantation.

The claim revived a long-suspected possibility: that despite family tradition, Dickinson may never have been taken to Maryland at all. At the time of his death, Nashville had not established an official city cemetery. It would not have been unusual for a prominent family to bury a relative on their farm. Some began to suspect that Joseph Erwin, rather than sending his disgraced son-in-law away, had chosen to bury him quietly on his own property.

When the Erwin plantation was razed in the mid-twentieth century and the land subdivided, any such grave would have been forgotten.

Historians and local officials soon examined the Carden Avenue property. At first glance, it appeared unremarkable, an ordinary home in a modest subdivision. But in the front yard, roughly fifteen feet from the road, there was a rectangular patch of ground, approximately three by eight feet, where grass wouldn't grow.

Archaeologists were called in. Just beneath the surface, they uncovered a stone slab. At that time, officials elected not to disturb the site.

However, in 2004, ground-penetrating radar was brought in. Over the next two years, teams of archaeologists and engineers returned periodically, mapping anomalies beneath the yard. Eventually, an excavation was approved.

What they uncovered was an old, hexagon-shaped coffin box. Inside were human remains identified as those of Charles Dickinson.

More than two hundred years after his death, Dickinson was finally laid to rest — reinterred in a family plot at the Nashville City Cemetery.

Charles Dickinson

Andrew Jackson

Rachel Jackson

Joseph Erwin

John Coffee

John Overton

Thomas Overton

No. 1st Charles Dickinson

Sir,
    Your conduct and expressions relative to me of late have been of such a nature and so insulting that requires, and shall have my notice— Insults may be given by men of such a kind, that they must be noticed, and the author treated with the respect due a gentleman, altho (as in the present instance) he does not merit it. You have, to disturb my quiet, industriously excited Thomas Swann to quarrel with me, which involves the peace and harmony of society for a while— you on the tenth of January wrote me a very insulting letter, left this country and caused this letter to be delivered after you has been gone some days, and securing yourself in safety from the contents I hold you in hate a piece now in this press more replete with black guard abuse than any of your other productions, and are pleased to state that you would have noticed me in a different way than through the press, but my cowardice would have found a pretext to evade that satisfaction, if it had been called for. &c. I hope sir your courage will be an ample security to me, that I will obtain speedily that satisfaction due me for the insults offered— and in the way my friend who hands you this will point out. He waits upon you, for that purpose, and with your friend will enter into immediate arrangements for this purpose— I am &c.

    May 23rd 1806   Andrew Jackson

No. 2nd

General Andrew Jackson

Sir,
    Your note of this morning is received, and your request shall be gratified— My friend who hands you this will make the necessary arrangements— I am &c.

23rd May 1806.   Charles Dickinson

Copy of Correspondence from Jackson and Dickinson
Photos Courtesy of Tennessee State Library and Archives

Charles Dickinson
Sir,
Your conduct and expressions relative to me of late have been of such a nature and so insulting that they required and shall have my notice. Insults may be given by men of such a kind that they must be noticed, and the author treated with the respect due a gentleman, although (as in the present instance) he does not merit it.

You have disturbed my quiet, industriously exciting Thomas Swann to quarrel with me, which involves the peace and harmony of society, for a while.

You on the tenth of January wrote me a very insulting letter, left this country and caused this letter to be delivered after you had been gone some days, and securing yourself in safety from the contempt I held you in, have a piece now in the press, more replete with blackguard's abuse, than any of your other productions; and are pleased to state that you would have noticed me in a different way than through the press, but my cowardice would have found a pretext to evade that satisfaction, if it had been called for. I hope Sir your courage will be an ample security to me, that I will obtain speedily that satisfaction due me for the insults offered, if it had been called for.

Know, sir, your courage will be an ample security to me that I will obtain speedily that satisfaction due me for the insults offered; and on the way my friend who hands you this will point out to you, for that purpose, and with your friend will enter into immediate arrangements for this purpose.
    I am,
    Andrew Jackson

Charles Dickinson's Reply

May 23rd, 1806
General Andrew Jackson
Sir,
Your note of this morning is received, and your request shall be gratified. My friend who hands you this will make the necessary arrangements.
    I am,
    Charles Dickinson

No 3rd   23rd May 1806

Sir, The affair of honor to be settled between
my friend Genl Jackson & Charles Dickinson esqr.
it is wished not to be postponed until the 3rd Inst
(say Friday) agreeable to your time appointed,
if it can be done sooner in order that no incon
-venience on your part may accrue, if you
can not obtain pistols we pledge ourselves to
give you choice of ours — Let me hear from
you immediately —   yrs   Tho. Overton
Dr Hanson Catlet   23rd May 1806
A copy of the   Prest.
original   — 1 —

No 4th   24 May 1806
Sir, I press you in favor of my friend
Genl Jackson for immediate satisfaction, for the
injury that his feelings had received from a public
-ation of Charles Dickinson, your reply that
it might not be in your power to obtain
pistols, in my note of yesterday in order to
remove every obstacle as it respected pistols, I agreed
to give you choice of ours, the other we pledge ourselves
to make use of For god sake let the business be brought
to issue immediately, as I can not see after the publi
-cation why Mr Dickinson should wish to put it off
till Friday — yrs   Tho. Overton
A true copy H Catlet

No 5th   May 24th 1806.
Sir, I have received your notes of yesterday &
this date, and can only answer, that it will now not be
convenient to alter the day from that already
agreed upon — I am sir with respect your Obt
                            Servant   Hanson Catlet
Genl Tho. Overton.

23rd May 1806
Sir,
The affair of honor to be settled between my friend, Genl. Jackson & Charles Dickinson Esqr. is wished not to be postponed until the 30th day; Friday, agreeable to your time appointed, if it can be done sooner. In order that no inconvenience on your part may accrue it you can not obtain pistols very far out of the way you have your choice of ours — let me hear from you immediately —
Yrs
Tho. Overton
Dr. Hanson Catlet
A copy of the original

24 May 1806
Sir,
I pray you in favor of my friend Genl. Jackson for immediate satisfaction, for this injury, that his feelings have received from a publication of Charles Dickinson, your reply that it might not be in your power to obtain pistols, in my note of yesterday, in order to remove every obstacle as it respects pistols, I agreed to give you those of ours, the other are loaded, and to make use of yours, for you sake let the answer be brought to you immediately, as I can not see again the publication why Mr. Dickinson should wish to put it off, till 30th day —
Yrs
Tho. Overton
A true copy
H. Catlet

May 24th 1806
Sir,
I have received your notes of yesterday and this day, and can only answer that I will not consent to alter the day from that already agreed upon —
I am Sir with respect your ob't serv't.
Hanson Catlet

N° 5th

On Friday the 30th Inst we agree to meet at Harrisons mills on Red river in Logan County State of Kentucky for the purpose of settling an affair of honor between Genl Andrew Jackson and Charles Dickinson esq — Further arrangements to be made — It is understood that the meeting will be at the hour of seven in the morning.

Nashville May 23d 1806   Hanson Catlett
                                Tho Overton

N° 6th

It is agreed that the distance shall be 24 feet, the parties to stand facing each other with their pistols down perpendicularly — When they are ready, the single word fire to be given, at which they are to fire as soon as they please — Should either fire before the word given, we pledge ourselves to shoot him down instantly. The person to give the word, to be determined by lot, as also the choice of position.

We mutually agree that the above regulations shall be observed in the affair of honor depending between Genl Andrew Jackson and Charles Dickinson esq —

                                Tho Overton
Nashville May 24th 1806   Hanson Catlett

On Friday the 30th Inst we agree to meet at Harrison's mill on Red River in Logan County, State of Kentucky for the purpose of settling an affair of honor between Genl. Andrew Jackson and Charles Dickinson Esqr— Further arrangements to be made— It is understood that the meeting will be at the hour of Seven in the morning
Nashville May 23 1806
Hanson Catlet
Tho. Overton

It is agreed that the distance shall be 24 feet, the parties to stand facing each other with their pistols down perpendicular— When they are ready, the single word fire to be given, at which they are to fire as soon as they please— Should either fire before the word given, we pledge ourselves to shoot him down instantly— the person to give the word to be determined by lot, as is the choice of position
We mutually agree that the above regulations shall be observed in the affair of honor depending between Genl. Andrew Jackson and Charles Dickinson Esqr—
Nashville May 24th 1806
Tho. Overton
Hanson Catlet

THE DUEL.

www.ingramcontent.com/pod-product-compliance
Lightning Source LLC
LaVergne TN
LVHW010217070526
838199LV00062B/4623